AN ANGEL DANCING

An original paperback, First published in great Britain 2009.

Publisher; New Edmund Publishing. Blackpool. FY1 6AX

Dedicated to my parents.
Joan and Charlie.

A special mention to all who helped in the production,

Adrienne Clater for the cover painting.

Enda Murray for proof reading.

Trina, Sue, Donna, Elaine and Rachel for encouragement.

Dale, Wes & Craig at
Print On Demand-Worldwide

Cathal O' Keeney, Was born in Donegal, Ireland.

At a young age, his family moved to Fermoy, County Cork. He was educated at Fermoy, C.B.S., Saint Colman's College and the Salesian College in Ballinakill. County Laoise.

It was at the County Laoise college he played a leading role in a school production and this paved the way for his love of writing and acting. For eighteen years he wrote and produced many stage productions around his home town, prior to moving to Lancashire, in the United Kingdom.

His main ambition was to write a fictional novel and finally after many years, We are delighted to introduce; AN ANGEL DANCING.

His biggest influence in writing comes from one of the most famous Irish writers, John B. Keane.

www.cathalokeeney.co.uk

Rivers of blood
A hatred so advanced
Morals in turmoil
But the Angel still danced.

Cathal O'Keeney

CHAPTER 1

As I gaze into the lights overhead, it reminds me of *that* day, the difference now is that the light seems dimmer, the silhouette is gone and the centre is but a dark void... 'Mister Rogers...' How could dirt be so clean, innocence so pure, youth so old and silliness so sensible?

Looking around the solitary ward, one would be forgiven for thinking, 'Here is a lonely man, ending his life in grey, dull surroundings,' However, one look at the single, red rose on the bedside locker, to me beautifies the whole world.

Even the inevitable pulse from the drip, cannot dampen the realisation that each one is replacing my natural pulse and eventually will win the race of endurance.

It is a strange scenario to think that I have lived for sixty years in a dull, normal, humdrum life, where nothing caused me any great affliction.

A life, where mundane jobs always kept me in 'The Black', then by contrast, to the past few months, which were full of learning, joy, elation and then grief. It is as if the, man above, allowed me to live the first part, just to prepare me for the latter.

I know now there is nothing further to live for and if there was ever a perfect time to die than this is it.

I wonder how the *sending off* will be? Oh, I know the arrangements; I have already set those up.

I can see Kathleen and Willie O'Donoghue, sobbing, hiding behind a tree, probably the only genuine mourners.

Old Frank, the gravedigger, no doubt will be there, leaning on the shovel, ready to swing into dignified action as to render soil on timber.

I can imagine Father Turley's eulogy, 'We commend to rest the body of Jonathan Rogers, a loving and caring man.' .... *As if.*

Who will shoulder the coffin?

Certainly not Mister Hawkins, the village mayor and certainly not any of the up-standing, members of the community council of Rahane.

Maybe no one else will turn up!

There is guaranteed to be one at least, even if to reassure herself that 'The Englishman' is truly gone. Yes, Miss Francis.

'The Viper Francis' as Willie O'Donoghue calls her... No wonder she has remained a Spinster... No I take that back Lord. All I will say is, if you will allow me to borrow your son's words, 'Forgive them, for they know not what they do.'

CHAPTER 2

If I were to place myself at the graveside of my dear wife Margo, this day instead of one year ago, my outlook would be so different, not because she was a bad person but because my 'yardstick' of measuring levels of love and the different degrees of love have completely altered. Life is a constant learning curve, the more you learn the less you know.

Our relationship was one of trust and togetherness. Overall, I suppose an adequate formula for marriage.

Margo was a survivor a true representative of self-dependency. This was evident when at the tender age of seventeen; she left her native Rahane, in County Clare in Ireland, to seek a new life in the metropolis of Brixton, London.

Even her name change from Maggie to the more anglicised Margo, showed her adaptability.

It is indeed factual to suggest that social and economic circumstances forced her emigration.

Together with two friends from her homeland, she took the 'boat' as many Irish had done before.

They were forced, to seek a better life on foreign shores. As one of her friends had a sister, already living in Brixton, the decision to adopt this borough as their new home was already pre-determined.

Margo came from a background of a 'typical' Irish, catholic, family, where truth and virtue had, by my standards an exaggerated value.

She was always soft spoken, but she could bring down a giant with her sarcasm, when disguised as wit.

To camouflage her frustration, she would sometimes mutter phrases in her native Gaelic tongue; my favourite was 'amadan', meaning fool, which was often directed at me. In fact, until one of her friends translated it for me, well into our relationship, I had thought it to be a phrase of endearment, because it was always disguised by a smile.

As for qualifications to enter the labour market, the Irish in general, seemed to possess more 'hands on' qualifications than we British did. Possibly, the skills they used on an everyday basis, from stone masonry through to needlework, made them more adaptable.

It was not too long before she found employment in the local clothing factory, making uniforms for our forces. I am certain that she did her job diligently, honestly, and never once complained of either conditions or pay. However, I am also certain that she hated the idea of being instrumental in producing items of war such were her pacifist ideals.

The one thing she constantly reminded me of throughout our acquaintance was that, she never hid her love for her homeland and constantly expressed her desire of some day returning.

'Ya know Johnny we will go back home when things get better that's for shure.'

Due to the amount of references she made about the country she had left behind, it instilled in me a desire to be part of this land and ultimately prepared me for my present situation.

Not a day went by without some reference to a fable or a landmark.

I, on the other hand had a less eventful childhood, born and reared by my widowed mother in a tenement, near the 'Elephant and Castle.'

My Dad died at the hands of the Germans, and as such, other than everyone referring to him as a hero, I never really remember him. My only access to him was through the tales and pictures, my mother had.

I left school early as I felt that the responsibility to fend for my mother outweighed the need for education. I worked for a local butcher on 'the bike', and this was to be my true school of life. Ration books were the order of the day and I quickly adapted to the implementation of pounds and ounces, as well as assessing the various 'sob stories' surrounding the allocation of the meat.

London was not what it is today, and travel time, was predictable. My 'beat' was quite extensive, it went well outside the boroughs of Southwark, and extended into the Brixton area.

I remember the first meeting with Margo; she approached me as a timid, inhibited young lady, typically thoughtful, 'Oh shure thers no need for you to be climbin' all them steps, 'tis only right that I meet you at the bottom, as 'tis for me your deliverin the Meat.'

I was smitten immediately by the broad Irish accent and the even broader smile.

Up to that point, I must admit that I had never even considered Ireland as a credible country. If one had asked me prior to advancing my acquaintance with Margo as to its location or proximity to the United Kingdom, I would in truth have struggled for an answer.

Her initial impact on me was so immediate that I offered to do the Brixton route any time the chance arose. I eventually asked her out and to my delight, we connected immediately. Margo treated every challenge with a degree of suspicion and because of this, our courtship lasted over three years.

We got married during the recession and despite the gloom of the economy, I was as content as an 'Arab sheik', because I had Margo by my side.

Margo's mother and father made the trip to the wedding and I can honestly say, that never before this time had I adapted so quickly to any two people. I cannot say the same for some of my fellow Londoners; they seemed to treat the Irish as a hated nation, and in fact, I was shocked on one occasion to see a sign on a boarding house 'No Irish or coloureds need apply.'

While on the other hand, I got the impression, that Margo's dad was not enamoured by us either, 'With the exception of you Johnny' he once said, 'I like the English a little, but I wouldn't ate a whole bag o' them.'

It was in a sad way a negative indictment of both cultures, that some sectors were quite uncompromising. Where people seemed to pre-judge and in fact mis-trust their fellow man.

Even at this early stage, I should have realised that a channel as narrow as the Irish Sea was so expanse as to create two completely different cultures. This applies even today and each is as guilty of blinkered vision as the other.

How strange it is to realize that events of so long ago, still re-visit ones mind as if it were only yesterday. Closing my eyes, I see vividly that youthful exuberance that constantly emanated from Margo's eyes, the dark auburn hair, the healthy honesty in her demeanour and her matter of fact indifference.

It is indeed strange to think that by today's standards, a young virile man should have gone into his twenties, without the certification of his sexuality.

Margo, fulfilled all my emotional needs to

the point where sexual gratification took second place. It also was the curtailment by Margo herself that killed any notion of 'Tom-foolery.' She had a clear concept of her Catholic upbringing. Although her church attendance was sporadic, she still carried through our relationship some of the celibate teachings of her religion.

Retrospectively I admired her for her various stances on social, sexual and political issues.

However, at the time they did seem a little unpalatable... It was at a very early stage in our courtship, that she introduced her love of the simple life, surrounding her upbringing in Ireland. She truly regretted leaving its shores. She stressed almost daily of the beauty and enchantment of the countryside and carried to her grave the sense of injustice in its inability to allow her to sustain a living and to remain within its shores.

She cited the weakness of the Irish economy at the time, but reading between the lines it was not difficult to assess her belief as to the main reason for such mass emigration.

She no doubt felt that more culpability was to be apportioned to Britain, for its eight hundred years of occupancy.

She recounted stories of the 'hedge schools' where the natives had to go underground to attain education, where society forbade them to integrate with their colonial peers.

She deliberated, enthusiastically, on occasions, about the victories achieved by Irish poets, bards and writers who succeeded in *beating the system,* by achieving fame and posterity, through their works.

'The pen,' she said, 'was mightier than the sword.' This was the weapon, she claimed, that eventually caused the downfall of the 'crown.'

She spoke regularly of an Ireland spurred by adversity, poverty and strife becoming the land of 'Saints and scholars.'

'Saints and scholars'… Boy how these accolades diminished rapidly, as I consider my current scenario.

I had not been in a relationship before so I failed to see or think it unusual for her uncertainty and mistrust of me as an Englishman. I can now understand the mistrust, of the English, which had been fuelled by years of suppression, and how it weighed heavily on her mind. The positive aspect however was that once those doubts had evaporated, the true Margo surfaced. Her qualities included purity, wisdom and knowledge.

I came to depend on her wisdom and it is true to say, that it would have been better for her to have survived me, than the reverse. Margo was a survivor, no situation would cause her to over-react or indeed make a rash decision.

I need only look at the trail of destruction,

that I have left since her death, in not only my own life but in the lives of all those that I have touched around me. This guilt is real, irrespective of how much I contributed to the situations.

Throughout the following years, we did not worry too much about the rationing, because as a butcher, I had first hand on the meat stock. I suppose it is fair to say that we were guilty of some crime or other but at that time it seemed more good luck than stealing.

Margo used to say by way of highlighting our good fortune, 'Johnny Rogers.'

'There's an angel dancing on your shoulder.'

Margo too, brought with her a fantastic ability to knit and I would say I was the best-dressed butcher in London. Proper woolly socks, hat, gloves, scarf and sweater. I did venture wearing woolly 'undies' for a while until it became unbearable, this was my excuse in later years for not having children.

The blitz and the bombing of London, at the end of 1940 even proved a strange up turn in our fortunes. The butcher shop was obliterated, but almost immediately, I got a position as a clerk for the conveyance company, handling the re-building of London. In time, I achieved the position of company legal secretary. A position I held until my 'Gold watch'.

Margo lost her Dad, quite early in our

marriage. He was dead and buried before the letter came to our home such was the delay in post.

When the word did arrive, we set off on the train, and boat, to visit and comfort Margo's Mum.

This was my first time west of Chelsea and it was a trip that was to make an impact on me for the rest of my life.

After the initial 'exploration', we made a vow to return to visit her mother at least once a year, a vow we kept, until her mother's death only some five years ago.

After her death, we visited the old cottage at least three times a year and Margo, paid an old gravedigger called Frank, to look after it in our absence.

Coincidentally my mum passed away the same year as Margo's did. I still do not know why but the two deaths coming so close eased the pain and helped us to share the grief and in this respect, we took a sort of comfort from the two tragedies.

CHAPTER 3

I must say that I grew a fondness for Ireland, that lovely, little cottage on an acre. It's possessive charm, the feeling of warmth, the clay window ledges, the half door and then the big yawning open fire, it was not just a house it was a home.

It was situated on the edge of the little village called Rahane.

The village itself only has a population of eight hundred people. The expanse of the village however makes it quite difficult to comprehend as to where this small amount of people resided. It is essentially a farming community with land handed down from father to son.

The buildings of note in the village, all have a story to tell, starting of course with the public house.

It is called 'The Mountain Barracks' (as one can see the old English military barracks from the front door). The pub is owned and run by Mick Foley, a quaint little individual. I am not sure if he was a 'leprechaun' or a human. When one considers the prices he charges, he is well on his way to owning his own 'pot of gold.' To be fair to him, though he sits on the fence and never seems to get involved in any conflicts. This ethos is inspired by the realisation as to 'where his bread is buttered' as much as his scruples. 'The Mountain Barracks' also serves as grocery store and petrol station.

Further along the street is the Church, presently under the control of Father Turley, A grey haired 'bible basher', who delivers decrees rather than advice, whose morals are as strict as security at the Hitler household. One who still marshals the teen discos with a blackthorn stick and a torch. His plumpness always makes me think, that he would rather save your dinner, than your soul.

Almost directly across the street, from the church, is the police station, as for the local policeman, or Garda, as he his known in Ireland, Father Turley makes him look as stern as a party planner at 'Butlin's.' His name incidentally is Mick Coskin, in truth a lovable rogue.

The next property of note is the dispensary, the home of Doctor Howard, (I use the title doctor loosely as he is not too often available, when a doctor is needed. He spends more time in the land of oblivion than reality due to his severe drinking problem).

Who would help if he was to suffer some accident? and in truth, he is the most likely accident victim in the village. It is the classic, scenario, how does the snowplough driver get to work?

The final commercial buildings in Rahane are the old and the new schoolhouses, the former now used as the community hall and when occasion arises as the courthouse.

The latter is the current school, run by the previously mentioned, Miss Francis. The less said about her the better, other than I once heard her described as 'the prettiest man in town', such is her abuse of ugliness.

Control of the affairs of the town are in the hands of the Community Council with the Mayor Mark Hawkins as head, when I say as head I mean precisely that, as the rest of his followers are as near to headless as the proverbial chickens. The linking attribute to the unified stance of the people in 'power' in the village is that they are all third generation natives, even the village doctor, is in fact a first cousin of Miss Francis, and the term 'blow-in' is regularly used to ostracise the enemy.

All the above character assessments are retrospective, had I known their 'true colours', then I would have re-thought my move to Rahane.

CHAPTER 4

The amazing thing that prior to the death of Margo's mum, every time we returned to Rahane, the locals treated us as royalty. A stop off at the 'local' always started with a free 'tipple', a welcome from all and invitations to christenings or weddings, even if the parties were un-known to us.

Whilst imbibing, Foley was guaranteed to summon his son to, 'Take the bucket and sponge and go and wash Mister Roger's jeep.'

I often heard the locals openly refer to us affectionately as, 'The English man and his wife.'

It was this open expression of acceptance that made me wish to end my days in such a foreign shore.

Things changed somewhat after Margo's death. Possibly the thought that land 'fought back' from the foe, was once again in 'John Bull's' hands. There is little else makes an Irish man more possessive than *Mother's green earth*.

Never will they forget their deep-rooted fear of history repeating itself with tales of eviction and land stealing by the gentry.

Irish history tells us that at first occupation some eight hundred years ago, that there is an area west of the river Shannon, known as the Burren, where the land is only made up of acres of limestone rock.

A General Ginkel, who was chief commander of the invading British forces, reported to the tyrant, Oliver Cromwell, 'There was not a tree to hang a man, no water to drown him and no soil to bury him.'

To this report when stealing the native land, Cromwell gave the Irish the option to go and live there or to be killed.

The immortal option was to 'Hell or to Connaught.'

These actions and the many other stories of plunder do not; to my mind justify the possessiveness that remains today. It is many a farmers driving ambition that his heir will protect the homestead as if it were still under threat. I have actually heard of land owners described as 'poor', when in fact they had holdings of fifty or sixty acres of land.

Maybe living in London has made me realise how valuable, in monetary terms a piece of land is.

At Margo's graveside on the day of her burial, as I stood there grieving for my soul mate, Hawkins approached me and said.

'Sorry for your loss Sir, and we will miss seeing you around the village, now that you have no more need to come here.'

'Leave it to me,' he continued, 'I will make sure you get a fair price for the ould cottage and we will put flowers regularly on Maggie's grave. So you won't have any need to come back......' I 'saw red' and assured him that he was right I would no longer be coming back...... as a visitor... 'I have decided to retire and move permanently to Rahane,' I said, 'as for the grave,' I continued, 'there is no need for you to worry as I will look after the flowers and it's up-keep, as I too intend to end my days here in Rahane.

Do you?' I asked, 'think that Margo was some sort of a dog that I just brought home to bury?'

Shocked by my declaration and by my fury, he reacted by stomping his foot in anger and then turned and walked away.

I can still see his face yet as he ingested my plan, 'he was like a bulldog chewing a wasp.'

This altercation had in fact nothing to do with my decision as Margo and I had spoken at length about eventually retiring here, just that Margo's heart failure forced my hand a little more prematurely than planned.

Another reason to want to stay was, that just down a path, through the trees from Margo's home, was possibly, the most beautiful, peaceful spot in the world. Right on the banks of the afore mentioned, river Shannon, (The longest river in the British isles), is a public walkway known locally as the SPRID, (in Gaelic this means spirit,) I assume so named as the folklore suggested that peaceful spirits cross here. An ideal place for true relaxation or indeed a spot of fishing, not that I was any great angler.

It did not therefore require a major debate within myself, to contrast this lifestyle of peace and tranquillity, with the other option of retirement back home 'midst the hustle and bustle of the Elephant and Castle.

CHAPTER 5

It did not take long to tie up the loose ends in London, and together with 'Pickfords' I sailed on the ferry for what was to be my last time, leaving the shores of old 'Blighty' behind. Many would think at the age of sixty it was silly to re-locate so far from home, but I must say in my defence, I really considered Rahane my home. After all, I felt it important to talk to Margo everyday. I also know now that I did not have an option, fate had decreed and I just followed. I was not a rich man, but I had enough money saved to afford a comfortable life, whatever its longevity.

My first day at the cottage was a most surreal experience. I walked along the outer perimeter, kicking up stones and sods of earth, as if to mark my boundary. I looked over my holding with pride and satisfaction. I knew even at this stage a new chapter was about to unfold in my life.

Reminiscing of course on the familiarity of various objects which triggered memories of the past, the old wooden stool that Margo claimed was the milking stool. I remember the silliness of her girlie antics as she sat down, on one occasion and said as she placed her hands in an extended gesture, 'Would Master like some fresh milk then?'

I remember her funny laugh as she picked a handful of chicken corn from a bag by the shed and made this weird 'clucking' noise as she scribed little tracks of corn across the field and watched as the chickens darted around her feet.

The more I looked, the more the various items unlocked the memories hidden in my mind. I could fully understand how a mother would spontaneously grieve at the loss of a child when she would recall instances in its life, when prompted by various items.

Pensiveness was the only true word to describe my feelings on that day, tinged firstly by elation, then sorrow and then again by satisfaction.

With old Frank's help, I 'did up' the old cottage. I put up a nameplate at the entrance gate, evermore to be known as 'Wyresdale' cottage. There was no particular reason for this name, maybe a mild statement saying 'The Englishman lives here.'

This time, however, no 'freebee' at the pub, a look of mistrust was often more evident than a smile, but at least most were civil; I knew to survive at the early stages, it was best to keep to myself as much as possible. It was as much a challenge for the locals to adjust to a new neighbour, as it was for me to settle in to a new environment. I either fished the river or walked the bank daily and in my mind, I convinced myself that I had inherited my own little piece of heaven. I walked with a 'swish and a swagger', soaking up the purity of the air and the slow pace of life. I thought, 'Johnny Rogers, You lucky bastard.'

My daily routine, started with a walk to the graveyard, then a call to the village, for the milk and bread. As to whether I got 'a tipped hat' or 'cold shoulder' en route did not affect me in the least. Some of the locals from time to time would greet me with, 'Top of the Morning to ya.'

Others would cross to the other side of the street, as if running from a leper. It regularly made me think however of the wisdom of my move but I knew that there was no going back.

CHAPTER 6.

One morning however, as I walked down the path, I saw a horse and a very young foal in my little field near the road.

'They must have strayed', I reckoned.

It was a pleasant sight and I suppose the lethargic side of me saw an effortless way of mowing the field. As I got nearer to the gateway that leads onto the road, I came upon a Gypsy type caravan, parked just inside my gate.

It was a rustic colour, with a canopy that was faded with age, it had two large rear wheels and a slightly smaller front set. Movement on its springs suggested that the wagon was occupied. I complimented myself in my lack of impetuosity, by presuming, that the horse was heavy in foal and they had to pull in overnight to carry out the birth.

I stood outside the 'wagon' and coughed loudly as a way of announcing my presence.

Then for a moment, I thought I was on the set of a 'King Kong' movie, as this enormous, un-shaven, longhaired man in one leap descended upon me from the wagon.

'What de fuck do you want?' was his eloquent request.

I was just as brave in my reply.... 'I ahh, I

ahh, …….I was just wondering, as to the nature of your business here?

'Look we comes here every year, at this time, we brings our childer to the school, the lady what owns this place, or old Frank the gardner, never bodders us and if you have any problems, with dat, den go make your complaint to dem. Now fuck off.'

He bellowed rather than spoke, his ranting continued without taking a breath and as he did so, his speech increased in speed to the point that it was completely incomprehensible, it was a good thing that I at least understood his opening tirade.

'Okay', I said, 'you can stay there,' as I interrupted him, when I eventually recovered my composure.

I would safely say that at my response, a feather could have knocked this 'man mountain' down. I went on to tell him the reason, there was no *bodder* from the landowner for many years was because she was deceased.

'I am the new owner and as long as you respect my privacy and keep the place clean, I have no problem with your stay.'

He raised his right hand to his forehead and gave what I would describe as a circular gesture; this I assumed was a sign of the cross, as he did so he moved his head forward in short convulsive gestures as if trying to read my mind. He actually trembled with trepidation. He was confused by my civility. I extended my hand and said, 'The name is Jonathan Rogers, and you are?' 'Willie O' Donoghue, Sir,' he stuttered, apologetically.

He then reached out and shook my hand in a sort of mechanical motion.

'Tank you, sir' was all he could reply.

As I went on my way, I still could not fathom what brought about the sudden transformation in this man. In an instant, he went from a raving lunatic to a docile child. In fact I was feeling quite chuffed with myself, I knew now how Jesus must have felt after dealing with Paul, on the road to Damascus.

CHAPTER 7

On entering the village 'proper', I was overcome by this eerie feeling, something was different; the school playground even seemed quieter. I looked around and nobody appeared in sight. It was like the closing scene from 'High Noon', all I was missing was the tumbleweed, the theme song and Gary Cooper.

I called to the 'Barracks' as usual, met Mister Foley as normal, but was met with 'eyes under the peaked cap'. I paid for my 'bits' and bade him goodbye. As I left the pub, I noticed an argument between Hawkins and Garda Coskin, down the street to my left. I knew by the feeble attempt from Hawkins to lower his voice that somehow, I was involved. Hawkins shrugged off an attempt by the officer to restrain him and made a 'bee line' to where I was standing, pursued closely by the officer, who was saying, 'look you are going about this the wrong way, Hawkins, let me deal with it.'

'You've had your chance, Coskin.'

'Mister Rogers,' he said, as he was still ten paces from me.

'who the hell do you think you are?'

'Your lot aren't Lord of the manor any more.'

Before I could ask for clarification, he continued.

'You! You! Are only in Rahane a few weeks and already you are stirring up trouble.'

'I knew things would happen'… I had to ignore him, by turning to Coskin. 'What is this all about?' However, before Coskin could speak, Hawkins continued.

'Your gate, Sir.' He replied.

'Well I don't believe it, all this fuss about such a little thing,' I replied, thinking that they were talking about my 'Wyresdale' nameplate.

'Little thing.' 'Little thing.' Hawkins shouted.

'Of all the arrogance, you'll be lucky if you don't find your precious cottage up in flames some night.' To confirm his threat he moved to within inches of my face.

'I will pretend I did not hear that Mark; now I suggest you calm down,' said Coskin. As he moved to my side.

On this instruction, Hawkins pushed us both apart in defiance and headed for the pub.

'What a hot head,' I thought to myself. 'Good job there aren't't many more like him in the village.' 'Now you get yourself home, like a good man, Coskin instructed, 'later on I will call up to check on you.'

With a gentle pat on the back, he left me to head home, still disbelieving what had just occurred.

As I passed the caravan at my gate, I was

suddenly shocked back to reality by a cacophony of voices all taking in unison, each trying to shout one and other down.

The group involved were, Willie O'Donoghue, whom I had just met, Father Turley, Miss Francis, Doctor Howard and a poorly dressed Lady in her mid thirties, whom I assumed to be Misses O' Donoghue. Plenty of expletives were colouring the air, being emitted by a male voice. I presumed from Willie O' Donoghue. A female voice, could also be heard, pleading, 'For God sake sstop'... I pretended not to notice and did my invisible man walk, in order to leave the scene as quickly as possible.

'Fools rush in,' and all that.

It seemed like I had only plugged in the kettle, when I heard the knock at the door. I looked to a Sacred Heart picture that Margo's mother had above the fireplace, and said, 'The quiet life. Huh! Give me back the streets of Elephant and castle, maybe anonymity was not a bad thing.'

When I opened the door, I was greeted by a combination of blank stares from the teacher, the Doctor and the curate.

I smiled a greeting in return, I do not know why, but I felt like an idiot because certainly none was reciprocated.

By the time, I uttered 'come in,' Miss Francis was already standing by the fireplace.

'Would you like a cuppa,' I asked, 'or maybe something stronger, I have a drop of

Scotch in the press?'

I saw the doctors eyes light up as to confirm acceptance but before he could utter a word. Miss Francis, spoke out, 'It has got to go,' she said. Father Turley nodded his head in support, like a nodding dog on the back window of a Morris Minor.

'If it means that much to you I said I'll have it gone tomorrow.' 'Anything for a quiet life,' I thought.

The tension in the room lifted like the steam from the now boiling kettle. Once again, I metaphorically patted myself on the back.

'Another well chosen few words, orator Rogers,' I said secretly.

Then I asked, 'but could you tell me why it caused so much upset.'

'I'll tell you,' volunteered Miss Francis.

'For the last six years they have come here, claiming their legal right to the sixty days of education. They disrupt the school, the town and'... 'Wait there one moment,' I intervened. 'What are you talking?'

So that is what Mister Hawkins, was talking about,' I realised, I chuckled loudly, as I reached for the proverbial penny from the floor.

'You are talking about the caravan at the gate,' I said, 'I thought you were talking about my nameplate.' I laughed again at my own foolishness. However, all I saw were three faces 'like smacked arses' staring back. Father Turley, responded by saying, 'I am glad you find it so funny, but your deceased mother-in-law, she started it. The silly old woman allowed them that space that first year, then after her death, when you were not here they still assumed they could park there. Old Frank was afraid to send them away so they got pushier and demanded to stay as a right. You were in London, so there was no point in involving you. Anyway I hope you stick to your promise and have them gone tomorrow.'

As he was talking they walked towards the door. 'Now good day, to you.'

They were gone! Was it my English accent, they did not understand? Did they not hear me explain my mistake? …Or did they not want to hear me?

I made my cup of tea, and I accompanied it with a slice of toast, I then lay on the couch and fell asleep. When I awoke, it was well in to the afternoon. I knew then for the first time that old age was catching up. The events of that morning were starting to burn me out. Even, this thought made my body respond in the affirmative, by sending a strange tingling feeling through my side.

Health wise I had always been blessed with above average health, not through any diligence of my own doing, but rather through care by Margo. She always worked diligently to make sure I was fed with 'proper dinners'.

'None of your greasy fish and chips,' she

would command.

I kept checking behind my ears for the emergence of gills due to the amount of cod liver oil, that she forced me to consume.

The ironic thing then turned out to be, that she ended up not taking enough care of herself.

CHAPTER 8

As a result of the deputations, opposing the gypsy family, I decided to go for a walk, to confront these 'demons at my gate' and to satisfy myself that I had not made a mistake that I could regret.

As I got near the wagon, I was confronted by a lovely scent of food. I approached with caution this time, calling well in advance. I am not sure if the old *ticker* could withstand two surprises in one day.

'Come on in, Sir,' said a female voice in the most peculiar accent I have ever heard.

'Come on in where?' I thought to myself. 'We are out in the open,' I walked around to the rear of the wagon. There I saw a woman, I now know as Misses Kathleen O' Donoghue.

'Danny, get up and give de man a seat.'

The little boy immediately jumped up as if awaiting any excuse to leave, 'I'm off for a while with Jimmy mama?'

He turned briefly and enquired, 'Will you be alright?'

He did not want or indeed did not wait for a reply. In two seconds, he had disappeared in to the hedgerow like a frightened squirrel. I looked and saw the young lad had been sitting on an old tyre. I dutifully sat down, and formally introduced myself. 'Jonathan Rogers, Mam.'

'Kathleen O' Donoghue, sir.'

'Sorry bout me husband, dis morning sir, she continued, but he don't mean no harm, tis not eaasy fightin every day for a space to sshhtop. We don't do harm to no one sir.'

'Your a good man sir, I knew that from the minute I herd your voice sir.'

She went on to tell me that, she enters the two school going children into the local school at this time every year.

'Tis a government ting ya know, that as travellers, dey must stil go ta school at least sixty days each year.

S'pose tis no harm for dem ta lern de tree 'R's, sir,' ya, know…Readin, Riting and Ritmatic.'

She continued to tell me that her husband Willie, never had any formal education, and because of this he was confined to travelling around on horse back to the neighbouring villages, mending pots, pans or indeed any work that came his way.

'Tis a hard life, sir but shur arn't we happy.'

She astounded me with her 'matter of fact' acceptance of life on the road. She spoke about, the constant moving, lack of help, obstacles at every turn. The second-class stigma syndrome. As I listened to her, I was captivated by the sincerity of her words, the obvious manifestation of truth and the total lack of resentfulness.

'God knows if any person had justification for bitterness,' I thought... She condoned her husband's aggressive style as a means of defence for his family, 'Shur he's da salt of da erth behind it all. He'd die forty times rader dan let antin happen to me or da childer and one tings for sure, if you're a friend of Willies he'll die for ya.'

She went on to tell me that they had four 'lovely' children, Tommy, a seven-week-old baby, who is currently sleeping in the wagon, 'A great child not a moment of bodder on him.' Next came Jimmy, at three years old, 'He has da head of on ould man up on him, always in mischief, knows no fear, but always senses if somtin's not right. Although all dat is bodering him at de moment is his birtday, it's in a few weeks and we promised him a party.'

'Den der's the man of da house, Danny.' With whom I had just briefly met.

She said, 'he feels at seven years old, dat he is in charge of de house, when his father is not about.'

'Finally dere's *Da Princess,* Rosemary. We calls her Rosie. She is eleven,' apparently going on thirty.

She described her as a 'loner,' she said, 'the two boys are always tageder, but, Rosie I don't know what she does be up at; I worry a lot about her.'

She took time out to remove a pot from the open fire, 'family dinner.'

She said, 'rabbit, tis Willie's favourite, your land is full of dem, and not one of dem has *de Mix*' I know bout deese tings.'

At one point when she was tending to the food, I noticed a very pronounced glance, in my direction a sort of a piercing stare; I thought she was going to comment on, some physical irregularity on my face, but what happened next took 'the wind out of my sails.'

'You're a troubled man, Sir,' she said.

I replied quite in the negative, I reassured her that the locals had misunderstood my decision and that I would stick to my original promise to allow her and her family to stay.

'This decision was even more reinforced by our present meeting,' I said.

'No,' she said. I'm not talking about, dat, I'm sayin' inside, der is problems.......

How do ya feel?'

She reached over, before I could answer and touched my side; a spontaneous tear appeared in her eye. To say that I was hushed was the understatement of the year. She dried her eyes and said, 'Ya best go now Mister Rogers, me husband and de childer will be along for der dinner soon... God be wit ya Mister Rogers.'

'What was all that about?' I thought, 'how perceptive is this woman?'

It took me nearly two days to get over our

meeting and to convince myself that, everything was fine. I lost myself in some more home improvements and deliberately stayed away from the village, *Let sleeping dog's lie*, I thought.

CHAPTER 9

The following day, I confined my morning walk to a saunter by the river and back through the main entrance. On approach, I heard some voices speaking quite loudly.

'Oh no,' I thought, 'more trouble, but on this occasion I need not have worried.

The scenario was, there were three men standing in a circle, negotiating the purchase of the foal that was the offspring of the O' Donoghue's mare.

Needless to mention, the most vociferous of the three was Willie himself. Although it was none of my business, I could not help but stop intriguingly in such a position that the gatepost hid me from their view. The second man in the group was a very well dressed character who reminded me more of a Fleet Street banker than a horse dealer. He was impeccably attired, complete with, pinstriped suit, velvet cravat and a pinz nez. The other character was obviously the horse handler, with looks and brain to match. His entire contribution to the deal was a grunt and a nod of reiteration, to any argument put forward by the dealer.

'Now, Willie if that foal was a Colt instead of a filly, it would of course be worth a lot more money and I would certainly........'

Willie, intervened immediately, stomped his right foot and shouted, 'Shtopp .. Sir,' He went on to quiz the dealer with deep verbal penetration.

'If I offered you an oil painting of my granny, how much would it be worth?'

The dealer stepped back with alarm almost standing on the foot of his Hench man, his eyes opened so wide with bewilderment, at the strange question.

'Well?.. Well?.. Well?'.. Willie probed.

Eventually the dealer replied in a confused state, 'How would I know, and what has that got to do with this foal?'

'Answer the question,' Willie insisted.

'If I brought you here today to buy an oil painting of my Granny, and I tould you, before, you came here that it was my granny, and dat I also tould you, dat the price was five pounds, would you buy it, if you was an oil painting dealer?'

I listened intently, bemused and probably just as baffled as the dealer was.

'Yes I probably would, but what are you getting at?'

'Very simple Sir, if you came to buy a painting of my granny, the most stupad thing you could say is,' as he put on a silly accent.

'Well, Willie if that painting was the Mona Lisa, it would be worth a lot more money.'

'De fact is dat foal is not a colt, de same as

my granny is not a Mona Lisa, ya knew before ya came here what I was sellin and ya knew de price. So shite or get off the pot!'

With a little nod of his head, Willie stared at his prey with the satisfaction of a cat after milk. I could not help a wry snigger, both at the deliverance of the orator and the dumfounded reaction of the receiver.

There was nothing more for the dealer to do but count out the money and shake Willie's hand to both confirm the deal and acknowledge defeat to a better dealer.

As for me, I returned to the house, pondering what I had just witnessed, realising that the school of life is indeed the ultimate educator.

CHAPTER 10

Shortly after lunchtime, I spotted Garda Coskin, coming up the pathway. In a way, I was glad to see him, because he is probably the only person in the village you would want to meet if you needed a stimulus. I had spent many a night in his company over a few pints of 'The black stuff', on my various visits to Rahane.

I am certain, that as a recent, resident of this community, he too suffered the 'blow-in', castigation of some degree.

'How's it going, Johnny?'

'Fine Mick, haven't had a chat for a while.'

'No not since the night poor Maggie was buried. How time flies. I've been meaning to call but with one thing and another.'

'Yeah that's alright,' I said, trying to let him off the hook. 'Well you are here now. Fancy a drop?' 'Not supposed to while I'm on duty but ...You forced me.. Just a little drop though.'

As he was shifting from foot to foot, he reached above the fireplace and took down an old rifle that sat on two large horseshoe nails.

'Margo's mother would turn in her grave,' I suggested, 'if she saw anyone touch that old thing, it once belonged to her late husband,

Padraig; he was a staunch Irish rebel. In fact, many times Margo told me that if the old boy had known of her interest in me at the start of our courtship, he would probably have dragged her back from Brixton. Such was his hatred for anything English. It was only a slow simmering process that made me acceptable.'

'Aye,' Coskin replied, 'you are lucky that you did not see the wrong end of this gun then,' he joked.

He seemed to examine the weapon further as he continued, this is referred to as an auld Fenian gun, 'tis many a home still has one over the mantle as a memory of days gone bye, I'll bet with a little drop of oil, this thing still works,' He replaced it, to where it was and then lowered his eyes to the ground.

'Look John, I am really sorry about that incident with Hawkins, this morning...' I stopped him immediately.

'Forget it Mick, you have the hardest job in the world trying to make everyone happy.'

'Well that is part of the reason I am actually here ....don't know how to say this but is there any chance you could make it down the village tonight?'

I detected a rather apologetic tone in his voice. I remember thinking; he is trying to make peace.

'No I don't think so,' I replied, 'it's possibly best to stay out of the village for a while, with this bit of ill feeling, that is going around.'

'Oh come on,' he begged, 'Maybe facing up to them is a tactic they won't expect, you know the average I.Q. of some of them in the council. Sure if they were shot for having brains, they'd die innocent.'

We laughed …maybe this was just the tonic I needed.

'We'll sit in the nook and no one will annoy us,' he suggested.

'Oh all right then,' I agreed, 'see you around ten o' clock then.'

'You might, eh, eh, try to make it for nine, if you could.'

'Okay,' I said, 'nine it is.'

Off he went with a sort of a schoolboy skip; he shaped up to kick a clump of grass but missed by a mile and nearly fell on his pants. It was like a scene from a Charlie Chaplin movie.

I definitely felt much better within myself after this visit. I started to believe that maybe because of the intensity of the previous conflicts there is now nothing left to dispute. I thought that in the wider scheme of things, How big 'a mountain' I was making of all this. The invitation of Coskin was the energizer I needed to ridicule my fear of 'the villagers.'

CHAPTER 11

I made an extra effort to clean and smarten myself up, prior to my infiltration of the natives. I found myself singing and washing at the same time, 'Maybe it's because I'm a Londoner,' So with my head held high I charged into the 'Barracks', Like Gene Audrey at the *batwings*, not caring if I was met with stares from all inside.

Even on a quiet Saturday night, Foley was guaranteed to have the local session players, *Fiddle* Hickey and the *Bodran* Milward, playing away in the corner. Then propping up the bar one would always find, 'Dan the Man', known far and wide for his stories all-starting with, 'In me father's time.'

The night in question was so different though, not even the cat sat by the fire. I walked across the sawdust-covered floor, and noted that I made the only set of footprints thereon. My first ridiculous thought was, 'am I hated this much that somehow word of my visit had preceded me and as a result they have all stayed away? Alternatively, had I stepped aboard the Maria Celeste?'

Even Foley had jumped ship, the only occupant was his daughter Rachel, a pleasant shy girl. She sat looking intently into the fire. She was reading the latest edition of the 'Rahane Gazette.'

'Where is everyone?' I asked.

Without answering, she deflected her eyes towards a poster on the wall. I followed her guidance and dutifully read;

TO ALL RESIDENTS OF RAHANE, AN EXTRAORDINARY MEETING WILL BE HELD AT THE OLD SCHOOLHOUSE THIS COMING SATURDAY AT 9 P.M.SHARP

I asked her what was this meeting about, but quite abruptly; she buried her head again in the publication as if pretending to not hear my question.

I naively wondered what was so *extraordinary.* I looked at the old clock behind the bar, to discover it showed, nine o' clock.

'I'm still in time,' I thought.

So I as a dutiful citizen, headed to the schoolhouse. I could not help wondering why Coskin had not told me about this meeting.

I walked into the room as discretely as I could, but if I had worn hobnail boots on a tin roof, I could not have achieved such a reaction.

At the top of the room was Father Turley. I am not sure, what he had been saying prior to my arrival, but he got a severe bout of amnesia at my entry. The silence was deafening and seemed to last forever, an aura of embarrassment was everywhere. People tried to bury their heads or pretend they were deep in conversation with the floor.

Suddenly like a cornered fox, Miss Francis jumped from her seat.

'Mister Rogers,' she said, 'it's good to see you here. We were just discussing some local issues and we have come to the distasteful topic of the squatters on your land. Now we have decided that a deputation from the village will approach them and tell them to leave or we will make a formal complaint, on your behalf, to the courts and then the police will move them.'

A rousing chorus, voicing confirmation emanated from the crowd.

'Tis for the best,' Father Turley chimed sheepishly.

'The best for whom?' I asked furiously.

I walked as I spoke. Eventually ending up, standing about a foot from *His Eminence*.

'Firstly, these people are not squatters; they have permission from me, the landowner, to stay.

In fact, I consider them my guests.'

I felt my mouth run ahead of my mind as I told them of the hypocrisy and the insincerity of their actions. Could they justify, I asked as to the true reason behind their bitterness. Hawkins stood up, as I knew he eventually would.

'We pride ourselves in our village and the people who live here. These *knackers* drift in and out, when ever they feel like it, with their dirt and their stench, they intimidate the locals, they demand their civil rights, they expect to drink in our pub, shop in our shop and even demand to sit with our children in our school.'

'What answer have you for that, Mister Rogers?'

I answered, with a forced calm that I never thought I possessed. 'I am surprised, that you do not exclude them from the church as well, or did you just forget to mention that?'

I looked at Father Turley, but I knew he was not going to respond.

Suddenly a realisation that I was out of my depth, descended on me. I just needed to look at the assembly to ascertain the fruitlessness of any argument or to expect any semblance of support. On the contrary, I noticed a 'Lynch mob' mentality. Only a few faces, in the crowd showed an air of support, most noticeably a small group sitting with Coskin. I knew then that this was the motive behind his invitation. Although to be fair to him, I know he did not expect such a xenophobic reaction from the masses, to my defence, of the travellers.

It was impossible thereafter to defend my stance as debate turned into hysteria. The motion for the prosecution flamed up on many occasion, fuelled by the odd interjections of Turley, Hawkins and Francis.

Even as I left 'a beaten man', some 'joker' shouted, 'Knacker lover.'

As I walked home, I tried to analyse the bitterness, 'Where does it all come from? Are their lives so devoid of genuine cares, that they feel a need to concentrate on bringing misery to others?'

I went straight home and sat down on the armchair, still aggrieved by the narrow mindedness of the mob. I was in this contemplating state for about thirty minutes, when I heard a car pull up outside. Within moments, the identity of the driver was revealed, as Coskin entered with a soft tap for clearance on the front door.

'I hope it is safe to enter', he joked.

'Johnny, he continued, that meeting did not go as I had anticipated and I want to apologise for putting you through the ordeal. I did not want to tell you about the meeting, because I felt had you known the content of it, then you would have stayed away. I further thought however that there would have been a bigger core of support for the traveller family and that our village rulers would have been the people to be opposed.'

'Mick, I assure you, if I had not attended that gathering, I would not have believed God himself, if he had told me of the bitterness and hatred that exists in people's hearts. I will further tell you, confidentially that if there was any way of exhuming Margo's remains I would move back to England, tomorrow.'

Coskin knew how serious I was, but he also knew that at my time of life, all other potential avenues needed to be exhausted first.

He said, 'There was a threat in the room about going to the courts to get a removal order, I can reassure you now Johnny, that that was a spurious threat. It is impossible to have the state remove anyone from private land, unless it is in contravention of the wishes of the landowner, or unless they are carrying out a felonious act. So in short, if you do not want them removed, then the law is powerless. I urge you to think the situation over for a few days and maybe the council will realize you cannot be bullied.'

'I promise you Mick,' I said, 'that is probably the only reason why I am unwilling to walk away, because I think it is time for somebody to make a stand on this issue.'

Speaking aloud about the issue took away some of the pent up frustration and I found myself slowly calming down. Coskin stayed quite a while and we shared a bottle of friendship, before we parted.

After he left, I knew that from now on I was going to be far slower to expect people to react in the way I would expect. It was in fact troubling to me that I was so naïve in my trust of my fellow man, that at this late stage in my life I was still learning the fundamental, primal instincts of survival.

CHAPTER 12

Around this time and possible as a direct result of the extra confrontation, I started to get some moments of dizziness and nausea. It was no coincidence that the timing of such, coincided with my altercation with the villagers. Also preying on my mind were the remarks of Kathleen O' Donoghue.

I had by now resigned myself to driving to the nearby town of Killalloe, for my supplies. My only need to go to the local village would be for the fresh produce like milk and bread, even then I made these provisions last longer than they were meant to.

On one such shopping trip to Killaloe, I decided to visit a doctor, as I felt no harm would come from a routine check up. His initial diagnosis was of stress and worry, but in any event he took some blood and urine samples, he also spent a long time looking at my eyes, he mentioned a jaundiced colour of the whites of my eyes.

He instructed me to return in about a week when the tests results would return from Limerick general. I was not overly anxious about these tests, but all the same I felt it better to have an up to date analysis of my health.

The strangest thing was that because of this medical check, I could say I never felt better and all thoughts of ill health quickly receded. I made a conscious decision to spend as much time as the Irish weather would allow to sitting by the riverbank with my fishing rod and flask of coffee.

CHAPTER 13

It was just before noon, the sun was as high in the sky as it would be. The reflection on the river was uncomfortable. Any fisherman worth his salt will tell you all these factors were against successful fishing.

The catch in my net after three hours fishing even by the wildest fisherman's tale amounted to the contents of a domestic goldfish bowl. However, I felt totally at one with nature, and savoured my own company.

I did at this point wonder was I ever going to meet a companion or was I destined to spend my days with only Mick Coskin, old Frank and his dog as my friends. Somehow, I knew that if this was my destiny than all I could do was accept it.

My thoughts drifted to Margo and the way life was so different when she had been around. The slow ebb of the river created a hypnotic effect in my mind.

The emptiness of not having someone to talk to, the feelings of uselessness and loneliness intertwined. I knew I was too old to consider another mate as I feared the dredge of baring my inner soul to a new partner, a stranger.

The little intricacies of two people in a long time relationship take years to understand and indeed accept.

Then suddenly I was jolted by the sound of some twigs breaking very near me. I turned as if awoken from a deep sleep and looked behind me. From my low position on the riverbank, I found myself looking straight into the sun. Before my eyes could re-adjust to the sudden light change, I witnessed what I can only describe as a vision.

The scene was an image of darkness coming through the centre of a light, getting slowly larger as I acclimatised to the scene. As my focus corrected itself, I saw the silhouette of a person walking towards me, as if emerging from that light. It soon became evident that it was in fact a female. Her sexuality was confirmed by the dissipation of the light around the flowing, blue dress she was wearing.

A very soft and gentle 'hello' preceded her clear visible person. I immediately responded with a croaked 'hi.' After she stepped out of the glow and came down to where I was sitting, she introduced herself, 'I'm Rosie O' Donoghue. I didn't mean to frighten you,' she said, as she extended a hand of greeting.

Even now, I can still feel the purity and slightness of her grip. The very thought of that first meeting brings a torrent of mixed emotions, tears of joy and sadness compete against one another as they gently reach my pillow.

'You must be Mr. Rogers?' She asked rhetorically. 'I was just coming here to have a swim', she gestured with an old bundled up towel as if to confirm her intention.

She was an immature looking young girl, I recall her mother telling me she was eleven years old, however, she looked a more credible eight or nine. She had very round features, a little underweight, but the striking feature was her purity, as in the perfection of her skin, it was totally un-blemished. This visage gave her the look of innocence. She had very long, flowing, blonde hair. It almost reached to her waist. A pudgy little nose and small petite, rather oriental looking eyes. I was never a good judge of people at first sight, but something told me this was a very special, young lady. The other striking thing about her was that she had an amazing clarity in her speech, totally without the blemish and mispronunciation that her parents emanated.

We spent over an hour talking, but that hour seemed like one minute, as I was so transfixed by the youthful enthusiasm she displayed. Suddenly without any warning she stood up and walked slowly toward the riverbank, she reached down and with a scissors like movement of her hands, she lifted her dress up over her head and in one full, flowing, instantaneous movement, she went from clad to naked. She placed the dress delicately on the grass, then without looking back; she just dived gracefully in to the tributary. I had no time to make any sort of reaction, so swift was the entire manoeuvre. Somehow, I did not feel embarrassed as I knew that she had not felt awkward in her nudity. I watched her cavort in purest innocence, childishly screaming at the coldness of the water. I unfurled her towel that was by my side and moved it nearer the exit point, to the spot where her dress lay. Finally, she appeared her head rising in to my line of sight. The next moment she sat towel clad by my side.

'Mamma says, we should wash near the fire, but I prefer to swim to stay clean,' she said.

I was speechless at her matter of fact ness. As she dressed once more, she turned and asked, 'do you come here everyday?'

It sounded like poor chat up line from the *ballroom of romance*.

'Yes' I heard myself say, in a direct hope that she would visit me again, such was the joy her initial meeting impacted upon me.

'Okay then I will meet you here again tomorrow, if that is alright?' she asked. 'I will be a little later though, I have to go to school.'

Without realising it, we looked at one and other and continued conversing in silence, as if we were mind readers. Then without any further conversation, she left as silently as she had arrived.

That night I lay awake for quite some time

reliving that initial sight of her walking through the light, it was as if the light paled by her approach.

I asked myself, 'Was I becoming such a recluse that the company of an eleven-year-old girl seemed a cause for elation.'

I left it much later to go to the river the next day, but even then the time seemed to stand still as I waited for her arrival. Every time I looked in the flowing waters, I could see her smile.

Eventually she arrived, looking exactly as she had that previous day. This time I could see beauty on top of all the previous qualities she possessed. In hindsight, I recall thinking that there were traces of tears in her eyes, but whatever the reason it was masked by her apparent joy to see me, a joy I fully admit was reciprocated. She greeted me with a gentle hug that for me, made the wait worthwhile. She attempted to justify the gesture as an offering of gratitude, as she said, 'You know, Mamma and Dadda really thank you for letting us stay on your land, 'tis not everyone would do this for us. I hope someday, we will all be able to live without always fighting for a halting space.'

She went on to speak about life with her family, about the rejection and bitterness from the 'Settled community.' Her words, flitting between alternate emotions of confinement and liberty, talking almost relentlessly, only stopping briefly to take a breath. I remained speechless throughout the exchange, totally overcome by her girlie exuberance and indeed her mature assessments.

It was only when I asked her about school that I drew a silence that in fact became uncomfortable. I could see that it was not just the school and learning, that troubled her, because I knew that she had the aptitude to *hold her own*. Instead of answering my question, she stood up and threw some pebbles in the river.

By way of a deflationary tactic, I asked her about the pony that pulled the wagon; this allowed her once again to return to her 'mile a minute' dialogue.

I was going to talk to her in advance of her anticipated swim as to the inappropriate nature of her actions. I was actually dwelling on a way of bringing up the subject without harming her innocence. Then as if to read my mind, she said, 'I don't feel like swimming today, Mamma gave out to me for swimming naked in front of you yesterday, she told me to say sorry.'

'But there was no harm in it was there?'

Before I could contemplate an answer, she said, 'Can we just sit and talk?'

As soon as I answered in the affirmative she actually lay down on the grass as if to show how comfortable she was in my environ.

'What is London like Mister Rogers?' She asked.

'Oh' I said, 'it's a bit like any other big city, a place where nobody knows your name, where nobody seems to care if you live or die.'

Retrospectively, this was a description of any where, if you looked at life through the eyes of someone who is a relative outcast in society. She however was so positive in her outlook.

'I'd love to visit it someday, do ya think I will Mister Rogers?'

I could see the images taking her imagination through varying degrees of fantasy, almost like Dorothy, on first visiting the land of Oz.

During the conversation, she rolled over and propped her head with her hands and started kicking up her legs, I could not help but notice that on the lower back of her thighs, just above the normal dress hem line, there were, some very nasty looking black marks. I am positive that these were not present, one day earlier, when she had completely disrobed for that impromptu swim. Although this sight worried me, I did not mention it as it was something she had to have been aware of.

She spoke at length about her parents and what really intrigued me was the ability of someone so young to evaluate the differences in character between them both.

'I really care for my Dadda, and sometimes Mamma is real hard on him. Last summer we visited my uncle Danny in Galway, and Dadda and himself went down to the beach one evening. Uncle Danny is a divil for the drink and he must have had a bottle of poi teen, or some other drink. Dadda did not want to drink it because he knew Mama would be cross, but on the other hand, he did not want Uncle Danny to think that Mama was the boss of him, so he drank the stuff. When he came back to camp, Mama tore stripes off him and made him sleep in the donkey blanket under the wagon. The following morning Uncle Danny called early and Dadda heard him just in time to spring out from under the wagon, otherwise Uncle Danny would have know he was told to sleep there. Uncle Danny said to him did Kathleen have a go at you last night and Dadda said, 'Not at all sure I am the boss of this camp.'

Uncle Danny roared laughing at him and Dadda only insisted more and more about him been the head of the house.

Then Uncle Danny said, 'if that be the case, I love the new hair gel you are wearing.'

'Dadda put his hand on his head to feel a big lump of axle grease, and then stormed off to hide, with the whole camp laughing at him.'

She was quite adamant however that they in their own individual way, her parents belonged together and indeed needed each other; it was as if their individual weaknesses made them strong as a unit.

She went on to speak of her own predicament and mentioned that when she turns sixteen, she will be expected, to go and live with a family called the Ryan's, near

Dublin. They have a son, with whom she will be paired with. She emphasised that she does not have the any choice but to accept him regardless of the fact that she does not like him. I asked her his name and she said Tony. Immediately I replied, 'Well this Tony Ryan is a very lucky young man.'

But she reacted quite defensively and said, 'No, no, no, Mister Rogers I just told you I don't like him.'

As if trying to make an effort to curb my perceived jealousy.

'I want to find someone that I, want to be with not someone the family picks. They can't make me like someone just because it's the traveller's way. I want someone who can bring me away from here. Her eyes lit up when she said, 'maybe to London even. Somewhere the traveller is liked not hated.'

Her speech moved from defensive to melancholy. 'Someone like you Mister Rogers.'

She turned on her side and again repeated in a much more sincere and reinforced mode, 'Yeah someone just like you Mister Rogers.'

I laughed at the absurdity of her words, but on the other hand, deep down I was flattered and surprised that she could not genuinely see the huge age gap between us and consequently considered me in the running for her affection in the future.

After some more effortless conversation she stood up and declared her intention to leave, then as if this young girl could not surprise me any further, She leaned towards me gave me a 'peck' on the cheek and whispered, 'Yah know Mister Rogers, 'There is an angel dancing on your shoulder.'

I looked in disbelief, my blood ran cold, I swear I saw a smoky image of Margo, I was powerless to react; I felt tears running down my face. My hands were sweaty and yet icy cold.

CHAPTER 14

The following day, I took an early morning stroll, still contemplating the previous day's events, my mind in a spin, and my morals in turmoil.

I called to the wagon to make some effort to explain to Kathleen O' Donoghue, the happenings of two days ago. As I got there, she was just leaving the wagon with a gallon can in her hand.

'Mornin' sir, she greeted, 'just headin out to pick some blackberries.'

'Misses O'Donoghue,' I replied 'I just want to….'

Before I could utter an other word, she put her index finger to my lips and said, 'You're a good man Sir, a good man' Then just walked away as if I did not exist. Nothing further for me to do but head back towards the cottage, completely unsure if I had been exonerated or admonished.

My pensiveness was abruptly halted by the sound of children giggling in the distance. As I got closer, I recognised little Danny O' Donoghue. As he saw me coming along the path, he ran towards Me with a ray of exuberance only seen in children. 'Mister

Rogers, Mister Rogers, Jimmy has found a bunch of little kittens, little baby kittens, they are in the ditch over here, Mister Rogers, come and have a look.'

I did not increase my speed, but my initial thought was what a strange place for a cat to give birth. When I got to the spot where Jimmy was kneeling, I momentarily froze. I was confused, never before had I such little time to calculate my next move. Jimmy knelt there; with one of the little animals in his hand…amazingly the mother remained watchful but strangely un-perturbed. I was probably the most stunned of all.

'Jimmy' I croaked, trying to stay calm. 'Give the baby back to its mammy.' 'Good boy Jimmy… put… the…. baby…. back.'

I watched helplessly as he gently returned the sibling to nurture once again beneath its mother.

As soon as his hand had withdrawn, I grabbed him very sternly by the shoulder, and knocked him to the ground.

'Why did you do that, Mister Rogers?' A shocked, Danny requested.

'Do the two of you realise that is not a cat nor are they kittens, these are rats.'

They both looked at me in amazement, as if I had two heads. Jimmy dusted himself off and asked 'so what?'

'De Mammy knew I wasn't gonna hurt dem' in the most matter of fact way that only his innocence could comprehend.

As I walked back towards home, I suddenly stopped in my tracks, and thought of the more global picture.

'Thank God for mothers, their intuition and their understanding.'

CHAPTER 15

Many days past and each day brought more reason to live, I am ashamed to admit it, but I was visiting Margo's grave less frequently, perhaps a tinge of guilt was encapsulating me. As I sat by the river once again, I looked around at the beauty of the scene, I thought William Wordsworth was not so clever after all, anyone could pen an ode to daffodils if one took the time to sit as I was among so pensive a scene, surrounded by his 'golden' flora.

Suddenly a voice broke the solitude; it was Rosie, panting un-controllably.

'Mister Rogers, you must come quick, Dadda has been arrested, help him please.'

Without expanding on any further details, she grabbed my hand and with strength that I could not believe, she dragged me to my feet.

'Where is he now?' I asked.

'Down at the Garda station, the policeman said he was going to put him in jail, Mamma said to get you cause you will know what to do.'

I did not delay to enquire any further as to the reason for the incarceration. I just sat into the jeep and drove immediately to the 'Garda' station.

As I walked in I found Coskin, sitting

drinking a cup of tea. He was clutching the cup as if it were about to jump from his hand. The inside of the station was a single room with a counter separating the 'Day' room from the public area. The mess of the room, I assumed was not a reflection on Coskin's housekeeping. All the promotional pamphlets from the counter were lying on the floor, as was the typewriter and some of the walkie-talkie equipment.

'Thank God you are here John, I didn't know what to do, I was called to a fracas involving Willie and some local youths over by the church gate, Willie was threatening to kill the youths, so I had no option but to restrain him, but the moment I put the cuffs on him he really lost it. I brought him here and you can see even in handcuffs, I could barely overpower him.'

I could see clearly how shaken he was.

'Where is he now?' I asked.

Without getting out of the chair, he threw a glance towards the big red door in the lower corner of the room. I accepted his suggestive head movement to mean that it was in order for me to go through the door and find out for myself. The reason for the apprehension in his demeanour became evident quite quickly. I opened the door that led into a dreary unpainted corridor. Immediately I heard what sounded like a wounded animal in a hunters trap. It was an eerie baying sound. I looked through the 'peep hole' in the steel door to see Willie sitting wedged into the corner, sobbing un-controllably.

I had enough newly found insight into the traveller's way of life to recognise that incarceration for them, was equivalent to death row for us settled folk. Freedom was a vital commodity to the way of life of the gypsy clan, hence their need to live and move nomadically.

I went back to Coskin and asked what happens next.

'There is no way of contacting a judge tonight, and I fear for the safety of the youths that he was in confrontation with. Therefore, I don't have a lot of options but to keep him here, until I contact a judge tomorrow. At the moment I can't make any sense of what happened, he is in no state to talk and the youths are insisting that Willie did all the physical assaulting, although off the record I somehow doubt it.'

I pleaded on Willie's behalf, 'there is the possibility that if he is kept in that cell overnight you could have a corpse on your hands in the morning. To take away the liberty of a man such as Willie, could be so traumatising that self-harm is a real possibility. Could you consider my word, as sort of a bail bond?' I asked.

'I will make sure he goes straight home to his family and to not go anywhere near the youths or their families.'

After careful consideration Coskin agreed, but he made it clear that Willie would have to realise any infringement would taint any hope of being exonerated in this matter. Obviously if the youths press charges I will have to re-arrest him later.'

'I will do my best to calm him down', I said, 'if you will release him into my care. However, I did reiterate that I genuinely was convinced that he was in far more danger of harming himself, if he remained locked up in that cell.'

When we entered the cell, I can only describe the expression on Willie's face as one of total bewilderment. I have seen the same tilted, head movement and expression from a longhaired beagle, I once owned. Particularly when he would hear a sound that was alien to him.

Coskin tactfully handed me the key to the handcuffs, and like washing a three-year-old boy, Willie extended his arms without reservation. I still remember the redness around his eyes, where he had furiously cried. I wondered if the remorse was for his predicament or for his actions. Whatever the answer I knew enough not to ask, as any reference to the reason for his arrest could trigger an adverse reaction. I was in truth very curious to establish the reason for all of the 'goings on,' but it was enough to get him home and in the company of his wife and children in the interim.

When we reached the wagon, he rushed to the comforting arms of his wife and immediately he turned into a meek puppy, apologising profusely and trying to warble some excuse, which she too was tactful enough not to analyse.

I bade them farewell, happy in the thought that Kathleen O' Donoghue had the power to calm the fiercest of beings.

A few days passed and indeed tranquillity set in but one knew it was the calm before the storm, little did I realise the extent of the gale however.

CHAPTER 16

Coskin called to the cottage and asked me to accompany him to the caravan, as he was about to officially charge Willie for attempted assault. The youths through their parents, made an official complaint and as a result, he had no option but to take this action.

Coskin had the foresight however, to arrange bail and in my absence, he had put me forward as posting same. He did this knowing I would have no problem with this arrangement, but more tactfully, it eroded the volatile potential of remanding Willie in custody again.

I assured Willie that I would bring him to Killaloe as soon as possible to find a solicitor, and arrange his defence. We both knew that seeking help from a local in Rahane would be a senseless exercise.

CHAPTER 17

The following morning, I did as promised, I collected Willie at the wagon and we headed for Killaloe.

On our trip, I was privileged to gain a different insight into this *big man mountain*. What a contrast to my first impression, on the day he descended from the wagon. Coskin once said, 'If you bought him as a fool, you'd be stuck with him.'

He came across as a clever man devoid of formal education. His method of speech was an articulate, confusion of pronunciations. His speed of diction was hilarious, there were many times when comprehension was deciphered, rather than understood. Never had I wished a trip to last longer than this, as I was so infatuated by the stories and indeed, by the way the stories were told. It was so unexpected from this man who had no formal education. I saw an insight into not just him, but to his culture. I realised for the first time that the traveller, or a *pavee* as he calls himself, is one of an indigenous minority.

I suppose they are an essential part of Irish society and have been for centuries. It is true that travellers have, probably a long share in history and the value system, which makes them a very distinct group. They have their own language, which is a thing that quite surprised me. It is called *Shelta*, which in turn has two dialects; *Gamin* and *Cant*.

He mentioned a possibility as to why 'settled' folk despised them; Story has it that a tin smith, worked on the assembly of the cross that Jesus was crucified on and before his death Jesus, cursed the tin smith; 'To walk the earth until Judgement day.'

As Ireland was such a Catholic country, it was plausible; he felt that this is where the initial seeds of discrimination were born.

They certainly have their own customs and more importantly, they have their own traditions.

I suppose by the very nomadic nature of their life and culture, that they are the people who helped to maintain in word and song the different incidents that happened in history. They brought the stories with them, as they travelled from one town to another plying their trade in an effort to simply maintain an existence for their families.

The sad thing of course is that the image of the traveller in Ireland today, can be described as one of social and cultural exclusion. The huge denial of traveller's cultures and the denial of their identity is indeed a tragedy.

The traveller's tradition is sometimes associated with vagrancy and then just naturally falls into the category of being criminalized. It is a terrible shame that traveller's crafts and travellers language is not recognised. Their values and beliefs are dismissed and ignored by a mono-cultural educational system. The travellers economy and work patterns are not acknowledged and if they are, it is with sheer contempt.

One constant theme was the repetitive mention of the stories, that his father and his grandfather relayed. Most of his learning came in the form of song and story and were all handed down from their forefathers, because writing was in the main beyond their capabilities.

So in this art they should be admired, as I am certain that these people are the central core of the survival of what is today known as Irish Traditional music.

Willie expressed to me on many occasions during that three quarter of an hour trip the different beliefs they have and all of them struck me as being genuine. There was nothing false, nothing insincere, nothing contrived, nothing to try to *screw the system*. All Willie wanted to do was actually help his family survive and enforce the principle of - 'Live and let live.'

He mentioned of course about the marginalisation encountered, not just this week or last, but from the day he was born. Life was a complete battle against the system, a system that they seemed to be forced into, when in fact one which they could equally live in parallel with.

It was quite amazing to hear him talk about some of the things, that I had not even considered; he mentioned that he is in essence a gypsy. He mentioned that throughout history, gypsies were a much-feared group, when in fact their only crimes are self-sufficiency, nomadic movement and self-expression through words and song. He mentioned that as a race, their movement and principles were feared through ignorant misunderstanding and as such, they were castigated as lepers.

'Look at the millions of Romany gypsies the Nazis killed,' he said, 'their only crime was that they were different.'

He went on to mention a little known, fact, more than double the numbers die in childhood than their settled counterparts. Those who do survive, do not live as long either, that is simply because of their way of life. Not being accepted by society makes their living conditions very harsh with few facilities and services.

Of their beliefs, he mentioned that if they were parking their wagon over night, they would never park across a gateway where on the other side of the road was another gateway. They believed that this was important to allow spirits freedom of movement.

It was also quite amazing and I suppose

reassuring to me, that he accepted me enough to confide in. I feel certain that some of the things he was talking about, had he aired them to others, would have received a more sceptical, or indeed a very cynical reception. It would definitely be misconstrued to appear as if he were putting forward a case as to why prejudice and discrimination has played such a large part in the segregating the two communities.

He further mentioned of course about the education and he spoke of the system that forces the children to attend a school where in fact he knew himself that they were despised and bullied. Life was very difficult for the children. He was amazed that even children as young as six and seven, were already tainted with anti- traveller feelings. It was not unusual, for young Danny to return from school and mention that he had been called either a *Pikey* or a *Knacker,* by children of his own age. He also mentioned that at least the boys were not as impressionable as girls were. He said, 'Kathleen is sure that Rosie does have it rough some times, dat's why I went ta meet her on de day of de fight.'

This gave me the opening to probe as to what happened on that day that culminated in his arrest.

For all his descriptiveness about our previous topics, he proved very dismissive on this present one. He diversified to talking about his wife, Kathleen. I am certain that once he had her approval for any situation, then he did not need to explain his actions to others. He openly admitted her wisdom and knowledge to be of a different league than his. It appeared that whatever, she decided he just went along with. He acknowledged that she had some superior intellect, not so much on an IQ bases, but on a feminine intuition type thing. Whereby, she knew and was very clear as to what was right and what was wrong. He mentioned that he felt she had some uncanny power to see beyond the physical demeanour of people, in fact he said, 'She could see straight into their hearts.'

He continued, 'Ill tell ya somtin for nottin, she says you, Mr. Rogers, you're the salt of the earth.'

I finally asked him, as to the logic of the traveller's way of looking at the world.

'Was there ever a way, that you could see yourself and your family remaining in one place and living in a house of bricks and mortar?'

Would you not think it more beneficial to integrate and become part of the settled community?

His reply was instantly negative, 'Mister Roger sir, a traveller living in a house, will always be a traveller, just as an English man living in Ireland will always be an English man.'

Travellers inhabit two worlds - the settled world and the traveller world. Settled people only inhabit one world and refuse to acknowledge the other. Therefore, the lesson I learned that day was, if tolerance were a ten-schilling note how worthless it would be, if it only had print on one side?

CHAPTER 18

When we reached Killaloe, I went immediately to the clinic. On my arrival, there were four people before me in the waiting room but as soon as I registered with the receptionist, she ushered me directly into the surgery, much to the dismay of the waiting queue. I met with a junior medic, who immediately asked me, 'Have you eaten any substantial meal today?'

I thought this an unusual salutation. 'Is this a surgery or a restaurant?' I joked.

'The reason for this question,' he said,' is that there is a short test we would like to carry out, but one has to be fasting for a considerable period prior to the procedure,' 'Well then, I am glad to say that my appetite of late has been quite poor and it was last evening since I had food and even then it was only a light snack.'

He instructed me to call back in an hour, if that was convenient. He further mentioned it would not be advisable to drive for some time after, as the procedure involved a local anaesthetic.

I had never thought to ask Willie prior to this if in fact, he could drive, but I felt certain even if we had to we could spend most of the day around Killalloo.

'Yes,' I said, 'there should be no problem keeping that appointment, that is the beauty of being in retirement.'

I asked Willie, when we were re-united as to his driving qualifications and I was glad even if, for convenience sake, that he answered in the affirmative.

We then found a local solicitor that Coskin had recommended. The company was called 'Paul Hay and Sons.' It was not long before we met a pleasant, gentleman, who appeared even some years my senior. Within moments, he had Willie; 'singing' like a lark, recounting the main background to the fracas.

It appeared that his wife feared somehow for the safety of Rosie and had asked Willie to go towards the school to meet her. As he was nearing the church, he noticed some youths, 'havin a go' at Rosie. His paternal instincts, took over and he man- handled the youths. I assessed at this point that he did use some excessive force. I deduced, also that it was luck for all concerned that the youths were more nimble and agile than their protagonist, otherwise I doubt if Willie would have known when to stop.

Although, I would not condone violence, no one knows how one would react if faced with a similar situation.

Mister Hay listened intently, then took details of the court date and said he would like to contact Coskin for his side of the story. He was careful not to comment on the projected outcome of the case, but he did reassure Willie of his firm's best defence.

Willie did make a relevant observation after we left the office, 'Ya see Mister Rogers, if you were not dere today, he woulda axed for money up front, cause normally dey don't trust travellers.'

We went for a short stroll down through the village, as we had some time to spare. It is indeed sad I thought that people do not realise the beauty of scenery on their own door step. Before us was one of the most picturesque scenes God could have created. On one side, there was an array of well-kept town houses and on the other was a lovely, clear-water, lake, with boats of all sizes and shapes. I was certain that people spend hundreds of pounds to visit here and yet people in the locality took it for granted.

On arrival back at the clinic, Willie agreed to sit in the jeep and have *forty winks.*

Once again, I seemed to be treated with priority as I entered the clinic. I was met this time by a more senior consultant, who told me that he would be carrying out a procedure, whereby he would be inserting a needle type object into my side and extracting a small trace of liver bile. He would then send the sample to Limerick and in a few days, I should call there for the result.

After disrobing, I was given the anaesthetic and the exercise was carried out, exactly as he had described. As he was 'operating', he asked about my functional habits and he revealed that the recent blood samples indicated a liver abnormality. This he said coincided with a swelling on my side and a jaundiced colour in my eyes. He did however mention that these symptoms are not in any way conclusive so until the sample he now had, was analysed he would not speculate any further.

In a strange way, I felt that the news was not unexpected and I think the original prognosis by Kathleen O' Donoghue had softened the blow, even though I had dismissed it at the time. I agreed to do as he suggested and at the time I gave little further thought to the problem.

CHAPTER 19

One good thing for me that resulted from the attack on Rosie and the subsequent defence by her father was that she did not attend school pending the outcome of the court case. The benefit of this was that she spent much more time in my company, or rather me in hers.

She became a perfect little servant, making tea, sweeping the cottage, getting logs for the fire; she even tried to bake some scones. When I say tried, even though her effort was better than any attempt I could make, they were over baked to the point that even old Frank's dog refused them. The one thing I learned, from this experience, was that one dared not laugh at her effort, because I saw a tint of her fathers temper coming through, particularly when one of the buns was propelled through the open, front door in frustration.

It was a total joy for me, to wake up each morning and to hear her singing as she walked up the driveway.

On one occasion, we walked together to the village. We collected the bread and milk at Foley's and went from there to visit Margo's grave.

Rosie was asking me about my former partner, when a group of youths passed and started shouting profanities at us and laughed as they ran away. Even though, Rosie thought that the derisory taunts were directed at her I am certain, I heard *English bastard*, flow from more than one set of lips. I immediately faced Margo's headstone as I said, under my breath.

'How much more should we take before we decide to leave this damn village? I feel the call of London is getting stronger, day by day.'

To which Rosie replied, 'I bet Mamma will let me go with you. Will I ask her?' she demanded.

It was too confusing to tell her that I was not talking to her, or indeed had I intended to include her. So I just replied, 'Let us give it a little while longer and see what happens, but certainly do not say anything to your mother at this time. Let it be our secret.'

I sensed Margo; laughing at the predicament I was getting into…Well I hope she was laughing.

On our way back to the cottage that day, I still remember with disgust, the curtain movements, the door closings and the huddled conversations as we passed by. I was determined to pass as if I was unperturbed, but the truth was that the walk to Wyresdale was more like a walk to Jericho.

The next few days, we isolated ourselves from the *outside world* and I took the time to show Rosie the finer arts of fishing. We laughed like little kids at the collection of tin cans and old boots that she hooked.

At one stage her girlie wit shone through as she said, 'Mister Rogers, for tonight's supper we will have, mashed potato, cabbage and rubber boot. How would you like yours cooked?'

It is in fact accurate to say, that every moment was a one to savour. I only hoped that she would be this happy for the rest of her life.

Each day we came to enjoy each other's company more and more, to the point that it was well after dark, on most evenings before I walked Rosie home. Each parting was confirmed by a gentle hug and a, 'See you in the morning, Mister Rogers.'

CHAPTER 20

The day of court finally arrived and it is fair to say that I was quite relieved because although it was not the *Spanish inquisition*, the unpredictability of the outcome did predominate my mind, as we got nearer the trial date. Although we hardly met in the interim, I felt it must have been causing Willie many sleepless nights. I knew, guilty or innocent, it would be proper closure for him.

I will never forget the tall figure of him waiting around the front door, clenching his fists and leaning every so often on his wife for the support he now took for granted.

The courtroom was a damp old hall, formerly used as one side of a schoolhouse, one could still see the Gaelic word for boys, i.e. *buachailli*, cast in the stonework over the entrance door.

At the top of the room was a large table with three chairs, strategically placed in different positions, two side by side and the other facing them.

The clerk, who was going through the caseload for the day, occupied the isolated chair.

The rest of the room was laid out as it had been the night of that, hatred meeting.

With the exception of a large 'Tri-colour' hanging on the wall, there was nothing to suggest it was a place of judicial importance.

There was by now an elite group of men and women, sitting slightly forward somewhat from the rest of the *audience*. These I perceived to be the legal *eagles*. I looked among them for Mister Hay, but did not immediately see him.

'Killaloo is fifteen miles away,' I thought, 'so he will be later arriving than some of the local solicitors.

Irish time meant that the eleven o' clock court, got under way at twelve fifteen, sharp.

The clerk ordered all to rise, 'The court is now in session, please stand for Judge Clapbad.'

The judge walked from the rear of the room to the table with the self-importance swagger of a heavyweight boxer emerging from the dressing room, 'All we were missing was the Fanfare.' I thought. The court was referred to locally as the 'petty session' and my heavens was this an apt description. The first case was that of a road traffic accident, involving a tractor and a donkey. This conjured all sorts of images in my head. I must confess that the speed of dialogue lost me after Garda Coskin gave his opening report.

The cases then got more serious, through un- taxed cars to eventually 'the Bodhran Milward' being fined for riding a bicycle, whilst under the influence.

Eventually the clerk called, 'Case number

twenty seven, justice is the case of O'Leary, Dougan and Ryan versus O'Donoghue. Mister Cribbs, prosecuting.'

At this point Willie walked forward, ready for the fray.

'We have no entry from a defending council, your honour.'

I remember looking around in a panic, 'What does he mean no entry; I was there when we clearly told Mister Hay of the court date.

'Did he forget?' I wondered.

'I take it then Mister O'Donoghue, you are defending yourself?' Clapbad, asked rhetorically. Willie stood forward from the crowd, visibly shaken, by this situation.

He blurted, 'I have axed Mister Hay, to be here for me. Will I phone him, to see where he is?' He pleaded.

'Maybe you don't understand the workings of this court,' Clapbad announced.

'The message is simple; we do not have an answer from any solicitor, entered on your file.

The onus was on you, to do this and you clearly have not done so. You cannot attempt to delay due process with your spurious claim. If any solicitor were to defend you, then he would have filed that intention. I do not know what game you are playing at but it will not work in my court.

'I am so sorry, if you will excuse me, your Honour,' I spoke out, 'but I attended the offices of...' 'Who are you?' Clapbed quickly interjected.

Then without waiting for a reply, he continued, as he stared directly at Willie.

'I am a very busy man; we have a huge case load today. Now at this late stage, your only options are to either, admit the allegations against you or defend the case yourself.'

'Well these are not very good, or very fair options', I thought.

Willie replied, 'Look judge the whole village knows what really happened that day.'

'Unless you intend putting the entire village in the witness stand, you can not say what they know, Now can we proceed,' At this point, I knew he was on a hiding to nothing, I remember someone once saying, 'He, who defends himself in a court, has a fool for a client.'

'Excuse me your Honour', was a call from the 'wings', it was the voice of Garda Coskin.

'We have a retired solicitor, in the court today maybe he would agree to defend Mister O' Donoghue.'

I looked around for the person to whom he was referring and suddenly realised that it was me.

I can vouch for the fact that Mister Rogers is a retired solicitor and maybe if Mister O'Donoghue does not object and Mister Rogers agrees then legal representation can be organised.'

'Me, a solicitor,' I thought. There is a big

difference between overseeing, building contracts and defending another human being.

I was not sure if Coskin was trying to help or hinder, but it sure seemed a better idea than poor Willie, trying to defend himself through tinted eyes of anger.

I agreed to make myself available and of course, Willie agreed. I then took my place at the front table.

Mister Cribbs opened the proceedings, 'This is a two fold case your Honour, firstly it is a judicial case, that if proven, the state calls for the incarceration of a violent and dangerous man, who by his actions caused grievous harm to three defenceless youths.

Secondly it is a case seeking compensation, for horrific injuries to the said, three youths, whose lives will never be the same again as a direct result of the afore mentioned barbaric act.

I will start by calling, James Dougan.'

Dougan was a sixteen-year-old youth, whom I recall Rosie saying was at the centre of the fracas, on that day.

Cribbs, opened by saying, 'Judge, I think it proper and it will save, substantial court time, by interviewing only one of the aggrieved youths, and if the court allows, the testimony he will give, should suffice for all three of the inflicted.'

Clapbed replied, 'Yes a good idea, that's if Mister Rogers has no objections?'

'I would like to hear the allegation first' I said, I knew enough not to allow one accuser, who could have been 'coached' on a potentially false claim. Dougan walked confidently to the 'top chair', he picked up the bible, as if it were his knife and fork at dinner and confidently repeated the swearing in process. After been sworn in, he started without any prompting, in the most monotone voice I had ever heard.

'On 27th March at half past three, meself, Paud and Allan, was walking home from school, we saw Rosie O' Donoghue, waitan, at the gates of the church. We asked her if she wanted us to walk with her back to her caravan. We were trying to be nice to her. She told us that she would not walk two steps with us as she said we were trouble, anyway she said that her 'boyfriend' was meeting her here.'

'Stop,' I said. 'It is obvious, to us all that you have rehearsed your little party piece.'

'Objection your Honour,' Cribbs interjected, 'I agree,' Clapbed replied, 'That is a serious allegation, you will get your chance to ask some questions, Sir, but this is not one of your fancy English trials. So stop interrupting.'

'I was becoming dubious as to the fairness of this court, but I knew that no further line of objecting would reap any rewards with this rogue, so I decided to allow Cribbs to do the maximum harm by showing his full hand before I could attempt to take it apart.

Cribbs, interjected. 'This boyfriend she was

to meet did she mention a name?'

'Yeah,' Dougan replied, 'It's, Mister Rogers', as he pointed directly at me.

The entire court laughed. I could feel a 'thousand eyes' cutting through me.

'Quiet,' Clapbed ordered.

Cribbs, replied, 'Sorry James, for the record, how old is this Rosie O'Donoghue?'

'Bout eleven or twelve, I guess.'

Cribbs gave me a glance of intolerance.

'Go on,' Cribbs replied.

'Well we laughed at the thought of an old man and this girl, being.... friends...... I mean 'tis not right, Judge. Straight away, she picked up a stick that had fallen off the tree by the church gate and started to hit us with it. Paud, fell backwards off the footpath as he tried to get away and when he was on the ground, she hit him four or five times. The next thing we see was blood on his face. Lucky for him she did not take his eye out.'

'During this assault, did she say anything?' Cribbs asked.

'Yeah, she kept shoutin' somethin about Mister Rogers and her and you are not to say anything bad about him like that.

Meself and Allan tried to control her so that Paud could get up. Just then, I was knocked to the path, meself, with a blow from nowhere. In our fightin' with Rosie, we didn't see her father Willie, jumpin us from behind.'

'He was mad, out of control; you know

what these tinkers are like, when they are after drink?'

'Objection your honour, you surely cannot allow these insinuations to go unchecked.'

'Mister Rogers.' Clapbed shouted, 'This young man is only sixteen years old and I am sure he is too young to understand the full implications of his dialogue. Some of us however have much larger moral issues, to contend with from what I am hearing. Now this is not the Old Bailey, so please don't interrupt again.'

'What happened then, James,' Cribbs continued.

'Well somehow in the we all ran different directions, cause he was too drunk to follow us.'

Cribbs then enquired as to the nature of the injuries sustained, to which Dougan listed out serious injuries mainly to Paud O' Leary, but also mentioned, 'we was all so shaken by de attack dat it will be a long time before our nerves will be better.'

'You had indeed a lucky escape' Cribbs responded.

'No further questions, your Honour.'

I stood up, knowing that everyone would laugh at any slip up that I was likely to make. I tried to appear composed.

Once again I asked Dougan to give us the story of the events, I emphasised that I wanted the account in his own words.

Again, off, he went in the same tone as before, 'On 27th March at half past three, me self, Paud and Allan, was walking home from school, we saw Rosie O' Donoghue, waitan, at the gates of the church. We asked her if she wanted us to walk with her back to her caravan. We were trying to be nice to her. she told us that she would not walk two steps with us as she said we were not good enough for her.

'That will be all,' I said, I knew there was no point in trying to get this rogue to change his tune, but it was damage enough I thought to hear his rehearsed speech for a second time. I allowed him to return to his seat and he did so with a swagger that indicated a sense of victory.

Cribbs announced that he wanted to call Willie O' Donoghue. Willie took the 'chair' as meekly as a lamb to slaughter.

'Now Sir,' Cribbs barked, 'Before the event that James Dougan described, where were you?'

'I was down at the dump getting some old metal for to repair a churn for a farmer up in Bird hill.'

'You lying toad,' Cribbs replied. 'I have two sworn statements, from regulars at Foley's that say you were in there drinking all day.'

'No sir I was not,' Willie replied. Then he looked through the auditorium, seeking his wife, 'Kathleen, I was not I promise I was not.'

'Never mind this Kathleen,' Cribbs demanded, 'Are you calling good citizens of Rahane, liars?' Cribbs retorted.

'No sir I...I' Willie said.

'That's better, now we are getting the truth,' he said, slyly, 'you then came upon your daughter, swinging a stick at these innocent youths, what did you do then?'

'She had no shtick sir; they were hitting her while she was lying on the ground. Yes I did hit out at dem before they did her some real harm.'

'So you did, hit them then. These boys are not much more than children, surely you realised you would do them a serious injury. But then you were out of control, with so much drink in you. It is a good job you are not facing a murder charge, you bloody mad man. Furthermore, it is a good job your daughter is too young to give evidence or be tried in this court, because it is obvious that she is as violent as you are. No further questions.'

I had to act fast to avoid Willie following Cribbs to his seat and pulverising him.

'Judge, I would like to reserve cross questioning of this witness, until I establish some further facts, from other witnesses.'

'What other witnesses? Is it not obvious to you that the facts are already disclosed?' Clapbed declared.

'Do what ever you have to,' he uttered dismissively,' but make it quick, time is precious.'

'Firstly, I said. I would like to call Michael Foley, proprietor of The Mountain Barracks pub.'

The entire courtroom was silent and stunned none more so, than Michael Foley, himself. He looked around the room for guidance, but every one looked elsewhere. I decided to go straight for the jugular.

'Have you a policy about serving members of the travelling community in your bar?'

'N…no..actual policy, I don't know what you mean.' He replied.

'Come now Mister Foley, if Willie and Kathleen O'Donoghue came into your pub and asked you for a drink. Would you serve them?'

'Objection, you're Honour' Cribbs interjected. 'The way Mister Foley runs his business is not on trial today, this is a totally unnecessary line of questioning and an intimidation of a good citizen of this town.'

'Sustained, Mister Rogers, he already told you he has no policy as such. Now accept his answer, Mister Foley is not on trial' 'Okay let me put it to you in a different way then, you see Mister Foley we have a newspaper reporter in court', I pointed to a gentleman, with a notebook in the first row.

'So are you saying that if any 'traveller' comes to your pub, you will serve them?'

I was relying on my character assessment of Foley, and his love for his 'green pound' to play this card, thank God I was right.'

'Well,' he said, 'A few years ago, we had a funeral in town and a large group of travellers were with the mourners, after a lot of drink a fight broke out and they wrecked the pub. It's not that I have anything against anyone in particular, but I don't serve them since.'

He blurted out his policy, before Cribbs or the judge could stop him.

'So, now, based on that policy, it was impossible for my client to be drinking in your pub on that day or in fact any other day. So the allegation that Mister Cribbs made is totally unfounded is it not?'

'Yes' he replied softly.

'Sorry I did not hear that?' I probed.

'Yes', he said once more, as he hung his head.

'Well he could have gotten his drink somewhere else,' Cribbs immediately shouted.

'Possibly, I said and no doubt you could produce witness who saw him there as well.' I replied. 'No further questions'... Foley stepped down, a dejected figure; however, he actually, *shot up* in my estimation as it would have been easier to lie to appease the masses.

This however exhausted my line of questioning. Not having the time to prepare for this case, I was probably going to get Willie an incarceration at best. My thoughts were to somehow, paint Willie in a good light, but I had a feeling that the non-arrival of Mister Hay and an antagonistic judge were not coincidences.

As I was just about to call Willie back to the stand, I noticed, Dougan and one of the other youths, smoking and just on cue I spotted him stub the cigarette on the bench top in front of him.

Immediately, I could not believe that such a valid point had eluded me throughout all the words that were spoken since the incident first took place.

With a new found enthusiasm, I sprung to my feet; I knew that if I handled this next part correctly, Willie's actions would be justified to some degree at least.

'For my next witness, your Honour I would like to call, young Paud O' Leary, one of the co-accusers.'

An eerie crescendo of silence fell upon the courtroom. O' Leary looked up at Cribbs, whom I assume had guaranteed his non-participation in the case and Cribbs immediately protested, 'Sorry you're Honour; I understood we had an arrangement to allow only one of the young gentlemen to give state evidence.'

Before Clapbad, could adjudicate, I said, 'According to young Dougan here, O'Leary seems to be the person most injured, in this fracas, so he stands to get the largest monetary remuneration, if such is due.. I think it is vital we hear from him directly as to the ferocity of his injuries, I am sure you will agree your Honour?'

Clapbad replied 'Yes on those grounds, I will allow the call.'

O' Leary was a timid, pale, under

nourished, scrawny looking youth. Sheepish in his demeanour and as it turned out in character as well. What did strike me as encouraging was the look of apprehensive guilt, on Dougan's face as I walked towards the youth in the dock.

'Now, Master O'Leary, you have been sworn to tell the truth, do you understand?'

Before he could answer in the affirmative I continued, 'How many cigarettes a day would the three of you smoke?'

Obviously taken back by the seemingly irrelevant question, he blurted, 'Only Jimmy and Allan smokes, I had a drag once and it made me very sick, sure I was coughing for days.'

'Based on what you have just told me, I am suggesting to you that there is every chance, that you will escape any blame, from the accusation I am about to make....if.. you... tell... me ...the... truth.

Look directly at me and tell me did you ever burn anybody with a cigarette, or did you ever see anybody been burnt?

Before you answer, let me remind you that you are under oath and the court looks very seriously on any person, no matter what age, if they lie or deceive the court.

As you do not smoke, there is every chance that you are not guilty of a horrible act called 'stubbing' that is to stub a cigarette on the skin of another person. I am sure you know what I am talking about.'

'Would you like to tell the court, how did Rosie O' Donoghue, get the burn marks on her thighs?'

Cribbs, again protested, 'Objection … judge these boys are not on trial, it's the traveller who is the aggressor.

Before the judge could adjudicate however, we were all distracted by the weeping youth sitting in the chair, and further distracted by the seepage running down his leg, over his shoe and onto the floor… 'I wanted them to stop,' he blurted, 'Allan was holding her down and Jimmy was lifting her skirt and stubbing out his fag on the top of her legs, where no one would see them, the traveller girl was crying her eyes out, Jimmy kept slagging her about the old man she had as a boyfriend. Her old man and her lover.'

'Objection,' Cribbs, kept trying to intervene.

'She was screaming with pain,' he continued, 'den her father came around the corner and he hit out, and I fell over, the others ran away and ….'

He broke down in a convulsive bout of crying.

I looked around at Cribbs, in time to see him bury his head in his hands.

Dougan was shouting both his innocence and his intention to kill O'Leary at his first opportunity.

In the entire melee very, few heard

Clapbed dismiss the case.

'That is enough, enough he said, case dismissed.'

When order was restored, I interjected, 'I hope either the state or the school will investigate the bullying that has been brought to light, today.'

As I spoke, I looked squarely at Miss Francis in triumph.

'Oh don't you worry the school will investigate,' she replied, 'Both this allegation and how you knew about the burns on the young girl, up under her dress line.'

That remark, despite Kathleen O' Donoghue's hug of comfort cut through me like a sword. Once again the entire courtroom was a melee, of voices, and the most vociferous of them all was an insane bellowing coming from a poorly clad middle aged gent in the second row, shouting, 'This is far from over, I'll make you pay for this,' as he pointed his extended index finger at Willie.

'Your little whore will suffer just you wait and see.'

Coskin told me afterwards, that this was Josie O'Leary, father of the young lad that was just in the 'dock.'

I could not help thinking about that final threat, nor have I forgotten it since.

CHAPTER 21

Whether in celebration, mourning, triumph or defeat, the Irish custom is to season such an event with a trip to the *boozer* and the day of the court ended in the same characteristic fashion. My initial thought was to head straight home, but I drew comfort from the fact that I had done a reasonable job and that maybe the fairer minded local among the rabble, would appreciate my stance. I also agreed to meet Coskin, after he called to the 'station' to sign off.

It was also better, I thought, to allow the O' Donoghue family to reflect among themselves on the implications of the day.

The atmosphere, I sensed was one of volatility, and even though the place was packed, I could not help but notice a group of four men seated in the corner, obviously talking about me, as was evident, by their odd glance in my direction. The circle of empties in front of them indicated that they had already consumed at least one round of drinks.

Sitting among this group was none other than Josie O' Leary, obviously still reeling from the humiliation endured by his prodigy. I for one was glad to see Coskin arrive. We sat together and talked firstly, about the day's events, but this soon became a spent topic as we recalled some old times. All the while, however, my attention was distracted by the *hate mob*.

Rachel Foley brought around sandwiches, and it was not too long before the *bodhran, and the fiddler* struck up a few chords. Every so often, the chorus of a tune like, 'The old bog road', or 'Noreen Bawn', would involve everyone singing in unison. The volume would kill any hope of conversation and one just had to sit and listen.

How poignant I thought, to hear them singing songs of emigration, where other nations accepted their forefathers in their droves. Yet here in Rahane, one Englishman is too many.

Daylight turned to dark, and nobody seemed to have any homes to go to. The atmosphere became less tense and possibly fuelled by *The Black Stuff*, more of the locals addressed me with some semblance of courtesy.

At one point I was even called to sing a song, but whatever chance they had of my speaking in a courtroom, they had no chance of any musical rendition. Attention quickly switched to Coskin and he duly obliged with his interpretation of 'Shaun South from Garryowen', a very strong rebel song. I was possibly the only person who noticed the words of hatred against the Crown.

'It's just a song', I thought, 'maybe I am

getting over paranoid.'

With these thoughts, I was prompted to look for my 'buddies' in the corner, however to a man they had vanished.

In the commotion of the request for a song from me and the subsequent request from Coskin, I did not notice them leave.

In a way, I was glad they had gone, as their very presence was quite intimidating and in truth, I found myself relaxing a lot more. It is funny that despite the obvious anti-British content in the words the clever thing about Irish music is that the beat 'draws' everybody in and I found myself punching the air just like the rest of them.

In a direct parallel to the night getting later, the volume in the pub got louder, every person wanted to be heard but nobody wanted to listen. I was no exception, and it was only by Coskin placing his hand on my forearm in a gesture of pause, that I noticed his eyes shift to one side of his head like a jungle animal listening for an impending attacker.

I suppose this quality of sensing impending danger was born from years of dealing with all types of situations and his instincts gave him the edge on trouble.

'Ya better come quickly, Mick' a tall rough looking figure suggested, 'There's some kinda trouble at the tinker's camp.'

I could not help but think, somehow Willie has lost it again, and this time it could mean big trouble.

CHAPTER 22

We walked quite briskly, towards the camp as none of us was in any state to drive. Coskin stopped briefly to get a flash lamp from his car. As he returned to our side of the road, a car set off from outside Doctor Howard's house and nearly collided with us all. It was heading in the opposite direction. I must say for a moment I thought it was a motorbike as it only had one working headlight. Coskin said, 'That's Peadar Scanlon's car, but I'll deal with that rogue in the morning.'

At this point, I did not realise the significance of this incident.

When we got to the camp, Kathleen was holding Rosie, who was sobbing profusely. As Coskin shone the torch on her face, it was obvious that she had been beaten. The top section of her dress was in tatters, and there were some large scratch marks on her shoulder and neck.

'Someone get the doctor', Coskin ordered. 'Now what the hell happened?'

At this point, we noticed Willie, staggering towards us holding his head, Kathleen, handed Rosie over to me and asked, 'Are you alright Willie? I thought we was all done for,' she said.

Willie was obviously more bemused than anyone was, and he too enquired as to what had happened.

'Kathleen replied, focussing her gaze directly at Coskin.

'We was just sittin here after puttin the small ones to bed in da trailer, I was singin a little song, when suddenly outa nowhere, dese men came runnin at us, dey had big sticks in deir hands, and da first ting one of dem did, was hit Willie full on da head. He fell like a sack a spuds, den two of dem grabbed my arms and pinned me to the ground. I didn't see anything else, sept I herd Rosie screemin. Den I herd one of de men leave out a much bigger scream and just as quick as dey came they wer gone. I reached over for Rosie and da rest you know.'

By this time, it seemed as if the entire population of Rahane had arrived to witness the 'show.' The only face I saw however was that of 'The Viper', although small in stature, her head seemed to be twice as big as anyone else's was. I did feel a little uncomfortable holding Rosie, so tightly.

Rosie then lifted her head off my chest and continued from where her mother had stopped.

'When they hit Dadda, and held Mamma down, one of the men, caught me by the arm and dragged me to the ground, I tried to pull away, but he hit me with his fist across my face and my head went all blurry. I remember him ripping my dress and as he was doing this, he kept calling me a whore. I felt him put his hand up between my legs, and he started to open the belt of his pants with the other hand. As I was near the fire I reached out for the poker and stuck the hot end at the man's belly, immediately he let go of me. All I remember then was him limping away screaming holding his tummy.'

At this point one of the villagers had returned, to report that Doctor Howard was out on a call, and could be away for some time.

Coskin immediately dispelled the mob and suggested, that they should all return to their homes.

Miss Francis was one of the last to leave and suggested that Rosie may need some medical treatment and that she could come to her house to await the return of the doctor.

'Deres no need for you ta worry, Miss, she's in da best of hands,' Kathleen O' Donoghue, replied, as they both looked at me.

'Not very well chosen words,' I thought.

'What do you suggest we do, Johnny?' Coskin enquired.

'Can you make sure the doctor calls, on his return? You might leave a message on his door.' I suggested.

'Why don't you all come up to the cottage?' I asked, 'No,' was the immediate reply from Kathleen, 'de small childer are all asleep in da trailer, so Willie and I will mind dem, but if you don't mind would you take Rosie wit ya and de doctor can see her dere?'

Before I could reply, Coskin spoke 'that is settled, an excellent idea and I will call for some more details in the morning.'

I was of course glad to take Rosie with me, more so when it was as a request from her mother. It was if I had a stamp of approval, despite the narrow mindedness of Miss Francis or anyone else. I knew nobody would cross Kathleen O' Donoghue.

When we got to the cottage, I took some of the driest turf I could find in the log box, I bundled up sections of an old newspaper and tried to get the fire lighting as quickly as possible. I gave Rosie one of my old shirts to replace the now torn and shredded dress. She quickly changed into the shirt and reappeared into the living room. I can still see her now as she transferred an elegance even to an old 'stiff collared' shirt. Her innocence and beauty just overshadowed any creature god had ever designed. At this stage, the fire was beginning to light and she sat down on the fire mat, close to the chair upon which I was sitting.

She crossed her legs, 'Indian style' and laid her still sobbing head on the side of my leg. I ran my hand through her hair and reassured her that all was now well. She responded by looking up at me as if to confirm my unspoken gesture. I just wanted that moment to last forever.

We sat for quite a while, both just staring at

the burning embers, without saying a word. We were both comforted by the thought that we were together and safe. After some time a knock came to the door and I went out to meet Dr. Howard who seemed to be a little under the influence, but I was glad he had made it.

Rosie walked with him into the bedroom and it was not long until he emerged alone. He had given her some sedative to help her sleep and mentioned that she had suffered a very traumatic experience.

He did confirm to my relief that she had not been physically harmed but we both knew that the emotional scars could be even more extensive.

He did not comment on anything about the actual attack. Therefore, I assume Rosie did not wish to re-live the incident. He just gave me some little bottle of tablets, I was not sure what they were, but he instructed, 'Make sure she gets them at regular intervals and do keep an eye on her during the night to make sure she does not go into some sort of frenzy or panic.'

He sat for a moment at the kitchen table, as he did so he managed to detract himself from his duties and return to his previous more drunken state.

Although I did not have much time for the doctor or his drunken binges, I agreed to give him some whiskey, after he tactlessly mentioned, 'A long hard day and how nice it is to be able to sit down and relax.'

I broke open a bottle of Powers and I gave him the bottle, a glass, and a small jug of water, as he freely helped himself.

We began talking about Rahane and the people, I even eluded to the narrow mindedness of some. I spoke of my decision to come from England and my reasons for being in Rahane. For a while, I actually thought he was listening to me, with a little bit of compassion and maybe understanding my predicament. I somehow hoped that he would mention the other side of my scenario to the town council and indeed to his family member, one Miss Francis.

However, after a while, he started to rant and rave as the drink 'kicked in' and then he started giggling and laughing. His speech became slurred and the meaning incomprehensible. He was muttering something about his job. He was voicing his grievance about having to leave his house at night. He mentioned something about moving away from Rahane, as he was fed up with the people and he admired the way I took a stand against them. I thought to a degree, if more were to think like him, then maybe, I could overcome some of the prejudice that exists in the town.

Having a conversation with him was a fruitless exercise, as he was waffling on, changing subjects like tuning a radio. Every so often, he would break out into uncontrollable laughter, as if something he had just thought of had re-entered his mind. I did mention to him that I would drop him home when he was ready to leave as I considered his driving ability to be very impaired. He looked at me as if to confirm my offer but instantly, broke into a sort of a weird, uncontrollable cackle and he said, 'Would you believe John Rogers, tonight has been the most eventful night of my life?'

I asked him in what respect, 'Was treating Rosie O' Donoghue standing out as being a highlight in his medical history?'

'No, where I was before that', he said, 'Do you know, I was sitting down by the fire listening to the radio, having a few well earned 'toddies' and the next thing there came a knock at the door and who was standing there? Only Peadar Scanlon, a local builder, and I said, 'What's the problem?' He said, 'Just grab your bag, come quickly and don't ask questions.'

'So', I thought, 'this is really serious', he brought me out to Josie O Leary's house, about a mile outside the village.

When I got there Josie was lying on the bed, naked from the waist down, with two of his friends, Donnie Murphy and Collie Roche, running in and out of the kitchen, with two big sponges of water and they themselves drunk as lords, spilling more on the floor, then they were carrying. In their rushing about, they were slipping on the water and falling over. Laurel and Hardy would have been proud of their routine.'

He started to laugh again uncontrollably. Then he said, 'They were dousing his testicles and stomach', and he screamin' in absolute agony and pain.

I thought to myself, 'This Doctor is losing it, if the thought of a person in pain is a recipe for hilarity.'

'So as soon as I entered', he continued, 'they just left the room, left me there looking at him. Apparently, he had been asleep, sitting by the fire, some time earlier and a can or something exploded in the fire and blew out a hot lump of coal. The lump of coal landed on his groin and burnt clean through his pants and well….. I don't know how to say this tactfully but he …..'

The Doctor stuttered and stumbled for quite a while, looking for some words to describe the scene.

'Let us say the best way to describe it would be, if he was an aeroplane he wouldn't be landing, anymore' I thought this was very vague, 'what is he saying?'

'Well let me put it this way to ya, I've often amputated a leg, I have often amputated an arm, but I've never amputated what I amputated off Josie O Leary tonight. I am afraid his days of womanising are well over. He once again returned to his laughter.

The seriousness of the event did not escape me however and it did not take any qualification from the Sherlock Holmes School of logic to figure out what had really happened. The doctor had given me the names of all the four characters that were at the pub that night. Hence, he has given me the names of the four people who attacked Willie O Donoghue and his family at the camp.

My immediate reaction was to go to Coskin and hand up the information I had just received, but then a devilish, satisfaction descended when I just thought in a sort of a way, justice has just been served. There is no way that any of the people involved would admit, as to where they had been tonight. Therefore, it would still be hard to prove. It was obvious that Josie O Leary was the instigator of it all. This was his attempt to make Rosie and her parents pay for the degrading of his son, in the courtroom today. All it got him in fact was a very severe amputation.

The *doc* was in no state to carry himself, so I put him in the jeep and dropped him home and on my return, I looked in on Rosie.

'What an ordeal you have gone through this day' I thought as I looked at the scars on her face.

I walked over and could not help myself giving her a soft kiss on her forehead; even though sedated I saw her cheeks expand to a comforting smile. I stayed in the room that night keeping watch from an old armchair that Margo's mother cherished.

My sleep was regularly broken by the movement and sounds from the bed. I knew that Rosie was re-living some of her traumatic moments of the attack.

At dawn, I got up as quietly as possible, and attempted to leave the room. I glanced back at the bed and again, exactly as we had first met I saw the bright light of the morning, hopelessly, trying to compete with the radiation of beauty, emanating from the pillow. As I pondered on the vision, a strange contracting feeling seemed to clamp my head. Was this some indication of ill health or an emotional, inexplicable disturbance?'

As Rosie lay asleep I pondered on the previous days events, particularly the remarks and accusations levied on her by her classmates and ultimately by her bullies. I wondered if these remarks would lead her to hate me, by considering me the cause of such venom.

As I looked at her in the light, I was quite proud of the fact that she seemed to like the accusations and indeed, it is possible that she, in her innocence, was the instigator of some of these rumours. It was as if the thoughts in her mind were truly of affection more than respect. Affection I must admit that I was devoid of since Margo's illness. I suppose I too started to feel sorry for myself, knowing that what ever lay ahead for me I would leave this earth a quickly forgotten man.

'However, that petite person lying on my

bed was a hell of a reason for me to want to live.'

CHAPTER 23

There is no doubt had I stayed in London; life would certainly have been different. This is the paradox of paradoxes, I was living in fast-paced London, but my personal circumstances were such that I was slowing down, then I move to slow paced Ireland and my life is now speeding out of control.

I went down to the Sprid to gather my thoughts and try to explore the reality of what was happening around me. I reached into the cold waters of the stream to sprinkle my face, in an effort to cleanse and to clear the confusion much deeper within. To try to find a descriptive word for my turmoil was indeed impossible. I could not truthfully say if my thoughts were impure, emotional or indeed just stupid. Maybe I was just too confused to be confused.

I certainly knew then and I do not feel any differently now, that this experience was one I did not want to end. It is almost like a junkie on his last piece of L.S.D.

'Whatever way it goes,' I thought, 'I must try to rationally, handle the future, but God knows how? I really needed guidance and assistance with this.

'Oh Margo, please help me, tell me what to do, tell me how to deal with what is happening.'

As I sat by the stream looking into the river, I failed to hear, the arrival of an audience.

A voice startled me and made me return to reality, 'No fishing rod today Johnny?'

I looked around and there was Coskin standing behind me, I looked through him like a lunatic through the bars of an asylum.

'Is this an answer from Margo telling me that I should confide in Coskin? Not sure if he is the man to talk to, if not, then who do I talk to?'

Coskin sat down beside me, as if reading my mind, he said, 'Are you alright Johnny?'

I said, 'No, I mean yes, Mick, just been an eventful couple of days. Any further news on last night?' I asked rhetorically.

'Any names on the culprits?'

Even though I knew myself who they were, and I knew what Dr. Howard had told me, I was just wondering if there was some way Coskin had pieced it together.

To a degree, I was not really looking for revenge because I felt that the good Lord above had dealt his own sweet revenge on Josie O Leary. No amount of earthly justice, would extract such a heavy price. He was certainly a loser in this incident.

'Well, let's put it this way', Coskin said, 'You know, I know and the whole village knows who attacked the travellers last night at the camp site, proving it is my dilemma. Nobody in the village will talk and they are coming up with a different stories as to how Josie O Leary has had a pain inflicted on him.'

Therefore, I told Coskin what I had heard from the doctor, and he said, 'Yes you are right, the doctor believes the story about the coal jumping out, but you and I know more truthfully, what has happened.

When Rosie stuck out the hot poker, she did not quite get him in the leg, she got him a little bit further up, in fact a perfect bull's eye or both eyes as the case may be.

The whole village, although they are not in anyway taking sides with the O'Donoghue's, they do sympathise with them. They realise that what O' Leary had intended to do, was as cruel and barbaric an act as to be abhorred.'

He went on to enquire as to the welfare of Rosie, and that in light of the recent revelations; he would have no further need to question her.

He did however mention as an afterthought, that he would not forget what had happened and that in time; he would extract some semblance of revenge on O'Leary. He got up from his hunched position and said, 'well I'll be off, some of us have work to do', and away he went.

The one thing that was certain, I always felt that after a time with Coskin, no matter what the occasion was, that I was better for the exchange. My mode of philosophical, self-searching had now passed and I headed back to the cottage.

As I pushed open the door I heard a rushed patter of bare feet on the floor in the bedroom, I guessed immediately that she had indeed recovered at least in a physical sense, so I left the front door open as to not make any further noise. I then walked quietly forward and opened the bedroom door. As I opened the door, I was just in time to see the blankets settling from their disturbance and Rosie lying in the bed, pretending to be still fast asleep.

'Well' I said in a rather exaggerated staccato, tone, 'the poor kid is still asleep, best leave her alone then.'

I turned deliberately towards the door, not really intending to leave, when a muted voice said, 'I'm not a kid.'

I then took up a position on her bedside and enquired as to how she felt. Without answering, she said, 'Mister Rogers' why did those men call me a whore?'

I looked at her trying to be as dismissive as possible.

'Those people last night were not fit to walk on the same street as you and as such, any names they called you do not even bear thinking about,' I told her.

'You are a very special young lady and I too, am sorry for calling you a kid', hoping that she would desist from the initial line of questioning, but she continued, 'Will these men come back, Mister Rogers? I did not like the way that man tried to put his hands on me.

I reassured her immediately, not wanting to allow her any time to dwell on the bad experience. 'No man will ever harm you again, Rosie not as long as I am alive.'

With these words she jumped up in the bed and threw her arms around my neck, and clung on to, rather than cuddled me, her warm breath gushing down the inside of my shirt collar, only stopping at my feet. I put one arm on her back and patted it gently, while the other hand filtered, finger by finger through her hair. This position gave me a sense of comfort as it did her. As I separated the strands individually, it was like a curtain slowly opening, but it turned out to be an opening I will never forget.

CHAPTER 24

As I looked through the strands of hair, I saw, standing in the doorway, the overbearing frame of Miss Francis. I pushed Rosie away quickly, with a movement that could be misconstrued as an admission of guilt. I decided my best form of defence was attack.

'Excuse me, but did you ever hear of privacy? Or at least have the courtesy to knock.'

'Privacy to do what, heavens knows what would have happened if I had not walked in,' she replied.

Her voice, not only had a sniggering tone but also one of satisfaction.

'It is as I thought your real reason for letting these knackers, stay at your gate' 'You without the company of a woman, for some time saw your chance with a defenceless, young girl.'

'You must be proud of yourself.'

She turned to Rosie and spoke in a horrible, condescending voice, 'As for you young lady, Rahane does not need the likes of you or your kind, and when Father Turley hears of what I have just witnessed, it will be a spell for you with the Daughters of Charity, locked away in their convent, and I hope they throw away the key.'

'What exactly do you mean, what you've just witnessed?' I enquired.

'You can't deny that you and that slut were in the bed together, and she naked save for a short shirt that barely covered her top and her age not long out of nappies.

Hell is the only place with room for the likes of you.'

She turned and walked to the front door; she put her hand on the handle and completed her exit by pulling the door behind her with utter vengeance.

Rosie and I looked at each other, bewildered both of us drawing different scenarios from what had just happened.

I tried to reassure her that all would be well, but somehow she knew that true conviction did not emanate from my words.

I suggested that she remain in bed and that I would go to her mother for some clothes.

Immediately I saw a change in her face, to this day I am not sure if it was a look of fear or thoughts of immanent exclusion.

'Mister Rogers, can I stay here with you?

For just a few days? I won't be any bother, I promise, please Mister Rogers?'

I wanted to answer in the affirmative, but I could not predict the future turmoil it could cause, I suppose the true coward came out in me.

'I will get your clothes' was the only answer

I could muster.

I went to the campsite, in a rather apologetic mood, wondering was I contributing to some global problem that would eventually cause Rosie more hardship and pain, yet confident in the fact that were the same situation to arise again I would not act any differently.

When I got there, I found Kathleen O' Donoghue, sitting feeding the baby. I discreetly coughed as I entered and without any further talk or salutation from both of us, I took my position on an old log stool. Our eyes met and I could see the understanding in her face, I knew there were topics that needed to be discussed but this was not the time.

'How's Rosie?' She enquired.

'Still shaken and very confused' I said.

'But she feels able to get up and potter about..... However, she needs some clothes, so that is why.... ' She did not let me finish, she just reached behind the spot where she had been sitting and handed me a small bag tied up with string.

'These will do her 'till I gets a chance at some washin', she calmly muttered.

I remember a strange feeling of guilt came over me as I turned to walk away, but I need not have worried.

'Mister Rogers' she called, 'Your reward will be in heaven, and God bless you.'

I got back to the house to find Rosie now

sitting beside the fire. No matter how she tried to disguise it, she had a smile as broad as a door at my reappearance. I have to admit that my heart fluttered at the exuberance. As I handed her the little bag I felt the touch of her hand brief as it was, to be a further moment to savour. She took the clothes eventually to the bedroom to change and as she did, I decided to go outside for some more firewood. As I lost myself in the task, a voice whispered from behind, 'Here let me help with some of those', it was Coskin, I was always glad to see him, but why so soon.

Thanks, Mick', I replied as I invited him inside.

Even before the kettle boiled, Coskin stated his reason for a second visit in such a short time, 'Johnny, I am sure you know I have just had a deputation from Father Turley and some of his side kicks. They are pretending to care for the welfare of young, Rosie. I am here truly as a friend to advise you to think deep within yourself as to the consequence of having her in the house with you. I know your predicament and you have my word that I will not get involved in any action that will go against your wishes, but you have to know that they are trying to get some way, to remove her from here and to ultimately remove her entire family from Rahane.' he continued with maximum sincerity.

'I truly hang my head in shame at the

narrow mindedness of some of these people.'

I could see his anger was genuine, 'It is a horrible indictment of the bitterness that exists, when I can not get a lead on the people who carried out the attempted violation of this young girl. While at the same time I have all these *do gooders*, trying to move a peaceful family as if they are outcasts.'

I invited him in for a cup of tea, as a gesture to calm him down. I knew that if he continued getting madder, he would only do himself some harm.

Rosie had the tact to go into the bedroom as we entered, she realised that our conversation would be curtailed in her presence.

'Mick, I have a situation that I am comfortable with and I feel controlled within myself, Rosie is trying to come to terms with what happened and she sees me at the moment as her friend, possibly her only friend and I am not going to be intimidated by a bunch of people riddled with hatred.

As you correctly said, 'why not ostracise this group of men who deserve to be hung. Are there any righteous people in this village? I ask myself.'

Coskin was now back to his sombre self and he smiled as he said, 'The only thing that has happened since is that there has been a funny side, if there can be a funny side, to Josie O' Leary's predicament.

Now that the news is out as to Josie's motives at the camp, I believe that it will only be a matter of time, when a swell of opinion will go against him, I heard the kids have a change to their skipping song and calling him Hitler. Because according to the myth, Hitler had only one ...you know what and they are singing Josie O Leary now has none.

I heard that Johnny Milward was in Foley's last night, talking aloud, with his famous chat up lines, after a few drinks, he said to Dan Roche, 'Dan did you hear that my dog was rooting through the bins down at the doctor's house the other night and he got two meatballs and a sausage', and the whole bar erupted with laughter.

Then Dan added his two pence halfpennies worth, by saying that he understands that the Rahane choral society this year don't have to find a tenor to sing the lead songs, that Josie O Leary is singing much higher than he used to sing.

'In fact I am also certain,' Coskin continued, 'that the three other characters who were with O' Leary in the attack, have completely disowned him and that in itself is a good thing, because the four of them together were nothing but trouble. All they needed was a bit of drink and the damage was just severe.

My only concern here of course is that Josie O Leary could react adversely in some way. I just hope he realises his mistake and curls up and goes into his shell. Somehow, I am not too sure.'

He walked around in a circle towards the fireplace.

'Call me a sceptic' he said, 'I have a bad feeling about all of this.'

As he spoke, I thought it very poignant that he reached up and pulled down the old gun from above the fireplace, twirled it around and just put it back on the nails. I noticed him shrug his shoulders and said, 'Johnny, I'll be off, take care of yourself man.' With that parting word, he just dropped his cup on the table and left, as if some idea had just entered his head that required urgent attention. I too looked up at the old gun, was he trying to tell me something?

Should I place the old gun at the ready, in anticipation of some reprisal? Alternatively, was I reading too much, from his words?

'Forgive me for being so stupid I thought to myself.

Before I could deliberate much more, my little friend emerged from the bedroom, dressed in the same simple dress that she wore on our first meeting that day at the 'Sprid.' As I looked at her, she reacted defensively, 'You don't like my dress, do you?'

'No its not, I mean the dress is fine, it's just, you look....

My mind was still back there at the riverside, not fully attentive to the situation at hand. In any event, I never had the presence of mind to say the right things, when confronted with a request from a woman, as to how she looked. It was always a scene that I handled with the tact of a bulldozer, breaking eggs.

'I will tell you what I will do; tomorrow I must go to the hospital in Limerick, for my test results, what would you say if I offered to buy you a new pretty dress, while I am there? One that really will make you feel good, and help you put these last few days behind you. Would you like that?'

Immediately her eyes brightened up and I thought for the first time in my life I had actually said the right thing.

'Great' she replied, 'what time are we leaving?' 'We' I mumbled, 'Em, em half past eight.' Was the only reply, I could muster.

'We had better clear it with your mum first though', I suggested.

CHAPTER 25

I thought of myself as an early riser, and so it was that I had the fire lighting by seven o' clock, in an attempt to make the cottage seem welcoming before Rosie got up. However just as the first, glowing ember started to overcome the morning dew, the front door opened and in she ran as if it was the middle of the day.

'Where have you been, miss?' I enquired, 'I thought you were still in bed.

'You said we must ask Mamma, if I could go with you today to Limerick. So I did. She said of course and that it was foolish of you to be asking,' 'Mamma also said something about, calling to see her when you get back to let her know how you get on.

Are you sick Mister Rogers?' was her perceptive enquiry.

'Cause if you are I can stay here and look after you.'

I am not sure to this day if an affirmative answer would have been more suitable to her scheme.

'No I quickly replied but it is no harm to get a check up every now and then.'

She just nodded acceptance as she continued fluttering around the cottage like a bird on a wire, making me a cup of tea, putting another log on the fire and all the time humming softly to herself.

To see her in such good spirits actually raised mine as well. It is a quite an extraordinary fact that youthful spirit is infectious, having her around me made me feel twenty years old again. A bit like some sort of an age redressing drug. I honestly did not want that feeling to end.

I realised also, that this to her was a big adventure. Possibly the first time away from the nest, her first time in a vehicle not pulled by a horse and more importantly the first time, she would be the centre of attention with the bribe of a new dress. We both knew this was a promise I would not renege on.

The trip to Limerick, that day was the fastest trip I had ever taken in my life, not because of the speed or distance but because of the constant chatter of my companion, she hardly stopped to take a breath. She spoke of everything from a snow white horse to the clear blue sky. It seemed to me that her young life was starting at last … One very important fact struck me as I was with her; I valued for the first time the poignancy of thinking this moment in time is now and can never be relived again. What is happening here and now will never happen again.

How I wish just once life could stand still. Time will dictate that soon I will be old and feeble and this young girl will be a woman, thus is the fickleness of life.

Reaching the hospital in Limerick was no problem but finding the right clinic within, was more of a challenge. A wry smile came over me when I noticed that the department I had to go to was next to the mortuary.

Rosie sat in the jeep, fascinated by the pre select buttons on the radio; this was just another part of the adventure she was living.

When I eventually, got to the clinic, I did not have to wait long before the consultant, brought me to a little room, which contained only a cloth covered table and a side tray of some surgical instruments.

'I would like to take a further updated sample of blood for analysis.' He said. 'We need to establish a time frame of the infection.'

I for my part agreed to give the sample without any thought of the consequences.

'Can you come back in the afternoon or even tomorrow? As the results will not take long to return, because the laboratory is within the confines of the main building here at the hospital. He asked.

'Then we can give you a more accurate prognosis.'

At that time, there did not seem to be any concern in his voice, but that proved to be his professionalism in full bloom.

I left the clinic at that time feeling quite content within myself and I was in no way apprehensive about returning in the early afternoon for the results.

CHAPTER 26

There was a beautiful stillness about the morning, one felt the possibility of the day incubating a warmer afternoon and as we had time on our side, I suggested to Rosie that we take a trip in the jeep to a place that I once visited with Margo. A place we both pledged to revisit, alas for Margo it was not to be.

It was to a place called the Burren, in County Clare. The total excursion around this phenomenal piece of landscape could be completed in a few hours. I embarked on this adventure for two reasons, one to see if certain sights jogged memories of past pleasantries and the second was to spend some individual time with my new companion and assess her reaction to the unknown.

The Burren itself is likened in many publications to the surface of the moon, I am certain that I heard somewhere that the name was an acronym of barren, as indeed it more aptly describes the area. This barren image however does not in any way detract from the uniqueness and beauty of the region and on closer inspection; it is an area so full of hidden treasures that a stranger could pass it by, totally oblivious of its wealth or complexities.

Our first, mandatory stop was to the little village of Corofin and its tourist center, in order to arm ourselves with the guidebooks necessary to properly explore this, 'eight wonder of the world.'

Whilst I looked through the various brochures on the area, I gave Rosie some money to purchase ingredients for lunch from whatever source she could procure them.

Each pamphlet, I picked up, rendered similar descriptions, mentioning that the Burren is an area west of the river Shannon and bounded on its left side by Galway bay and the Cliffs of Moher.

The name Burren is from the Irish - bhoireann meaning a stony place. Its formation has lain unspoiled since the ice age and it is composed of karst limestone, the largest area of such in Western Europe. It goes on to mention that the area involved has an expanse of some two hundred and fifty square miles. It is a place of surprise and delight to botanists, archaeologists and ecologists alike. The area itself is very bleak in appearance with soil at a minimum.

However, it does have sufficient soil to grow a wide variety of the most unusual and rarest of plants, many of them strange bedfellows, due to the heat retaining properties of the rock. An amazing collection of alpine and Mediterranean species grow together throughout the area and it was while reading about these flora that I was intrigued to discover that in a little village just north of here was a perfumery that in fact extracts the scented oils from the sheaves of lavender and other plants that are native to the area. The bi-product is then made into perfume. I knew this would appeal to Rosie, so I decided to make it our next 'port of call.'

I was drawn to a well-written feature giving one comical warning about the trip, 'On the way towards the perfumery, one will encounter a winding down hill descent called the *corkscrew hill*, this road is so winding in fact that at various points thereon you will be able to see the back of your own neck.'

It was not too long before Rosie returned with a bag of goodies and she seemed genuinely excited when I told her of the planned itinerary.

I realised very quickly during the course of this day as to why Rosie was so interesting to be with. It was because she was such a perfect listener, not only did she want to know all the abstract information concerning the region, but also she wanted to know the how, the where and the why surrounding them.

At times, I felt a little like a tour guide as I repeated the information that the various brochures revealed to me. I felt happy and indeed proud to be able to convey this lesson to such an appreciative audience.

When we reached the perfumery, I struggled to keep up with the youthful athleticism displayed by Rosie, as she dashed towards the entrance.

My speed was further hindered by my need to identify all the varied concoction of scents and aromas that I inhaled, as I got closer to the building.

My young friend however had no such barriers and within ten minutes, she had sampled every tester from the hundreds on offer. I spoke at length to the proprietor, enthralled at the thought that an industry such as this could survive in such a remote location. Her rebuttal, however was most logical as she pointed out that it survived, because, of its location.

Rosie had by now lost herself completely in her own little world of fantasy, possibly believing she was some rich queen, with all the luxuries of the world at her disposal. She flitted around oblivious of any other person in the shop, like a bee collecting pollen in a garden.

I smiled to see her making attempts to pronounce to herself the various exotic names of the ingredients. It appeared the more difficult the word the more was the facial contortion. On one occasion, I had to laugh aloud at her, when she appeared to react with abhorrence at a particular description.

I caught up with her on her third round of the display and asked, 'Would you like one of them to take home?'

'Oh yes, can I really?' she gleefully replied.

She selected two contrasting packages and tossed them in her hands, as if guessing their weight. It was obvious to me that the reason these two were selected was more for the prettiness of the packaging than their content, but I knew enough not to mention that observation.

'Which one would you prefer Mister Rogers?' She enquired.

'Oh I can't chose for you,' I answered trying to be diplomatic,' I believe different people have different preferences, otherwise there would only be a need for one fragrance.'

'But I want you to chose which one would you prefer?' She insisted.

I took each of the testers and very quickly chose one. To which she immediately commented.

'That was exactly the one I was going to pick too.'

I smiled an acknowledgment and complimented her on her choice. She sprayed some of it in the air trying to make it descend on both of us rather than just her. We paid for the package but Rosie declined the offer of gift-wrapping as she intended to open it as soon as we got to the jeep.

As we set off to explore further, Rosie's total concentration was on the little bottle clutched tightly in her hand. I did notice in my side vision a very erratic head movement as she looked at the gift for a few seconds, then looked at me for the same amount of time, then back to the bottle. This gesture was repeated for some time, to the point that I had to interject and tell her some more facts about the topography.

Even though she was listening intently, she continued to emanate an amazing sense of joy and satisfaction by smelling the backs of her wrists and every now again opening the box and spraying small little wisps in the air. I felt proud to be able to bring such joy to another human, such that I felt a tear in my eye.

It was probably the first time in her life that anybody even allowed her to be exposed to perfume not to mention her owning her own.

We then drove for quite awhile in the direction of a village called Kilfenora. The moment I saw the place name on a signpost I remembered Margo telling me of her late father's love of traditional music and mentioning that one of the most famous bands of this genre came from here.

At this point, the trip took an element of surrealism, as there were times when I glanced at my current companion and saw images of my former. At one stage, I addressed her as Margo, but thankfully, she did not hear me, as I was not sure how she would have reacted.

Before we got to the village however, I pointed out to Rosie a large collection of stones, placed meticulously as to form a dolman. In my own mind, I likened them to a mini

Stonehenge.

Even though they were some distance from the road, their presence was rather imposing.

As her eyes set on the large stone object, she shouted, 'Stop, we must get a closer look at it, can we?'

Her curiosity was so enthralling that I dared not refuse. I looked briefly through the pamphlet and informed her that this was a portal dolmen, dating back to about two thousand five hundred years before Christ.

'It was probably a formal burial place', I revealed.

'It has an unusual name, it's called Poulnabrone, that means in Gaelic, a place of sorrow. None of the brochures mentioned as to why it was so named.

All of them did however recount a similar tale of folklore, attached to the stone, which involved a girl called Deirdre, who lived many years ago, when Ireland was a monarchy. The Druids or the wise men employed by the king, prophesised at the birth of this young girl, that she was to be responsible for friends and families becoming embroiled in conflict leading to much loss of life. They warned.

'She will turn brother against brother, father against son, 'til all are no more.'

The king took this prophesy as a challenge and said, 'We will let her live and at the age of sixteen, she will be my bride, hence I can control her every movement and ensure she does not cause this anticipated grief.'

Whilst growing up however she befriended a boy of her own age called, Neasa, who for his part along with his four brothers, became an integral part of the king's warriors.

Over time, Deirdre and Neasa became so infatuated with each other that they could now allow the marriage to go ahead. The night before her wedding to the king, they eloped together and left word that they would head for Alban, which is now Scotland, to take refuge there.

The king sent many scouts to find her and to bring her back, but all to no avail, because they did not in fact head immediately for Alban, instead they hid on the Burren and nightly took shelter here under the capstone of Poulnabrone.

They did eventually flee to Alban and just as the druids had prophesised, some of his family supported his actions, whilst some did not and eventually a battle took place resulting in huge losses on both sides.

Rosie listened intently throughout the entire narrative; she sat transfixed to the tale.

Her culture and the story telling around the gypsy firesides made her a perfect listener. This was obviously a vital part of her learning process, to enable her to store such information for future recounting.

When I had finished she immediately opened the door and got out, it was as if the lesson had now prepared her to feel the physical vibes of the monument.

I suggested to her to wait until after we had eaten, but she just seemed anxious to continue, whilst the pamphlet, description was still foremost in her head. She suggested that we bring the food with us.

'We can have a picnic beside the stone.'

This I realised was another fundamental difference between, the traveller and the settled communities, the thought of eating 'al fresco' with a bleak, wind about to sour the atmosphere, did not seem over appealing. It was fruitless to argue, but I did take the precaution of putting on my overcoat, which lay across the back seat. My body temperature receded even further when I realised that Rosie wore only a light summer dress, with possibly little else underneath. Either the lack of creature comforts in her home habitat or her youthful exuberance had rendered her immune to the elements, but I did not enjoy such a luxury.

Rosie had already retrieved the bag of food and was heading towards the entrance.

In order to give tourists access, to this historical feature and to deprive farm animals entry, one had to scale a small man made sty. This was to enter the first of the two large enclosures, prior to reaching the dolman. I refer to them as enclosures, but it would probably be more accurate to call them large fields, but I find it difficult to refer to large masses of rocky underfoot, surrounded by man made stonewalls as such.

Even though Rosie was far more nimble than I was, she still allowed me to catch her around her waist, to assist her progress through this 'gateway'.

We were only a few yards into the journey when I felt Rosie's right hand grip my left, in what I perceived as a token of togetherness. I foolishly but instinctively looked around to see if anybody had witnessed this gesture of familiarity.

This I realised was a ridiculous precaution when I considered that we were in a remote location, 'miles from anywhere.' Thinking about it afterwards, I am not sure if I would have done anything differently, had there been an audience.

I will admit that I did feel a little uncomfortable on first contact, not because of any moral issue, but rather because it was an alien act for me to participate in.

In the many years that I had been with Margo, I cannot recall more than two or three occasions when we held hands. If any guilt did occur, it was knowing that Margo would not have approved rather than any social stigma. I am certain however that from Rosie's perspective, the gesture was totally innocent and it was her way of portraying gratitude for this current experience.

When we eventually reached the site of the

Dolmen, we were both shaken in wonderment as to how in fact the large capstone had withstood the forces of time and nature to command its precarious position on top of its supports. How it was placed there was also a mystery as hydraulic lifting equipment was rather scarce around two thousand five hundred B.C.

The air temperature by this time was getting noticeably cooler, but my companion was intent on sitting beneath the large stone, to have our picnic. I took off my coat to give some form of comfort beneath us, as Rosie opened the bag to reveal her purchase. The child in her came to the fore immediately, as she displayed the food.

'She didn't exactly think it through when it came to substance,' I realised.

All we had was loads and loads of strange silly looking sweets, lollypops and a large bottle of red lemonade. She did at least buy, two cups made of tin, to drink from, she referred to them as 'pandies' a term I was not familiar with.

'What the hell' I thought to myself, 'this was her day and I was not going to spoil it by being judgemental.'

I found it difficult I must admit, trying to eat some of these ingredients and give the appearance of enjoyment. Some of the items seem to explode in my mouth, others stuck to my palate and teeth, but the worst was a sweet she called a 'gob stopper', which was definitely related to the rocks that surrounded us.

As we sat 'neath the dolman and ate our *food*, It was obvious that the inclement nature of the Irish weather was about to reveal itself. Little did we realise how violent it was to become. In a matter of seconds, it turned from a teardrop to a torrent. We were momentarily trapped within the meagre cover of the dolmen. The ferocity of the downpour, sounded like a thousand bass drums and we found it difficult to hear one and other. The good thing of course was we both knew we were not in any mortal danger and that the likelihood was that the rain would rescind as rapidly as it began.

In the interim, we shared the overcoat as we huddled closely together. Rosie drew the parallel with Deirdre and Neasa from all those years ago. How ridiculous I thought for me to be compared to a brave warrior.

'I hope the rain never stops,' she said.

'Isn't this exciting?' She continued. 'Are you happy, Mister Rogers?

I confirmed my happiness by putting my arm around her and gently squeezing on her shoulder.

The silly thing about this gesture of happiness was possibly the most honest message I have ever expressed.

In a fantasy world, I would have wished for this moment to last forever and indeed, in my mind, it will. To put comparatives on my contentment would be impossible as this moment surpassed any other in my diminutive life. She interrupted my thoughts and said, 'You know we too could go to Alba to live and nobody would ever find us. Wouldn't that be fun?'

I laughed at her teasingly, but in a strange way, I heard a seriousness in her voice that to a degree activated, a pensiveness in me.

For the first time I must have felt a bit uncomfortable in her company. I would have loved to go back to that day again and delve into her perception of our relationship.

Possibly if I had truly understood her frame of mind, then the ensuing, repercussions may not have occurred. I know now I was on a big, selfish ego trip and should have known better. The affection she was starting to build up in her mind towards me was in fact becoming dangerous.

All I thought about was the joy of someone so young, beautiful and innocent, inflating my self-esteem.

'Oh, Johnny Rogers! What did you do?'

Our moment of intimacy was interrupted by the murmur of a diesel engine, combined by a swish of air brakes as a coach load of American tourists, pulled up behind the jeep.

Rosie emitted an almost reciprocal sound through her teeth, signalling her disappointment, at the ending of our solitude.

By now, the rain had ceased, to a degree that allowed us to rejoin our vehicle.

On the return leg of the trip back to Limerick, there were very few words spoken, as we were both in a nostalgic frame of mind, reliving the many wonderful moments of those past few hours.

I had to remind, Rosie, that immediately after my return to the hospital for the lab results, I would then complete my promise to purchase the new dress.

CHAPTER 27

It was early evening time as we found ourselves back at the hospital. This time however the setting sun tensed the general atmosphere and I got a strange eerie feeling as I entered that clinic.

It was obvious that the lady behind the typewriter was expecting me because she asked my name in a rhetorical fashion and on my acknowledgement; she disappeared into an adjoining room. Her return ushered my entry via another door on the opposite side of the room.

In this room, was a tall, surly man in a white coat.

'Come in Mister Rogers, and take a seat,' he instructed.

He had a folder in his hand and appeared to delay in reading it, as if once again to confirm it's contents.

'John, may I call you John?' he enquired. Without waiting for an answer he continued. 'There is no easy way to say this but those stitches you are getting in your side, ...well I'm afraid the results reveal that your liver is badly infected. You are suffering from a medical condition, called, ***cholangiocarcinomas***.'

He allowed these words to *sink in,* before continuing. Cholangiocarcinoma is, I am afraid an incurable and rapidly lethal disease.

The interval between your two blood tests reveals that the growth is too advanced and I am afraid no curative treatment is available. In lay-man's terms, so bad in fact that, it is pointless attempting any form of surgery, management rather than cure is our only action.'

I sat looking at him as if his voice was resounding in a different room, words that seem to echo down a tunnel. 'Are these words directed at me?'

'No this is some sort of joke, I only have a pain in my side, overexertion that is all it is, this guy does not know what he is saying.' I thought.

I tried to put every other spin on the situation, but then the real one finally hit home. As if reading my mind he produced a bottle of some liquid or other, 'Any time you feel the pain John, take a spoon of this, however there will come a time when even this will not ease the pain.' I know this sounds callous; however, I have to be honest with you.

'I am truly sorry, John.'

I sat still in the chair looking at the lotion and trying to ingest the true impact of his words. What he was saying, were words no man ever wants to hear, but I found myself accepting his diagnosis as definite.

'How long?' I blurted.

'Could be a few weeks, three months tops.'

He then left the room with a parting hand shake and said, 'Take as much time as you like here, if there's anything, Miss Dudson can get you. ... A cup of tea or a little drop, then you just ask.'

I stayed for a short time, looking out the window, thinking a thousand different things all at once.

A soft tingling on my shoulder broke my trance; I instantly placed my hand on the spot and said to my imaginary friend, 'Better make room at the ball for one more guest.'

Eventually I emerged from the doctor's room into the waiting room; I noticed the absence of the secretary from her desk. I suppose it was difficult for any person to look face to face with a person who is just about to complete the circle of life.

As I walked through the building towards the exit, my mind spun around trying to understand the point of life. Would my existence mean anything to anyone, had I achieved any thing? What was it all for? I reached a degree of loneliness, as I have never reached before. Would I meet my maker, or were all these Christian beliefs a load of old cobblers? What if there is no after life? Even if there is what credentials have I to enter with the righteous? I should be all right, I have never done much harm, but then neither have I done much good.

Depression was a real emotion as I realised that no one will shed a tear for me, nor can I confide in anybody. For the first time in my life, I needed someone to take me in their arms and cry with me. A lonely, condemned man on death row, but without a crime to answer for.

Just then, a crazy thought ran through my mind, if in fact I had doubts about an after life, than what was to stop me doing the most illegal thing possible?

Even if caught and convicted, I would be dead before sentencing. Weird as this may seem I actually, enjoyed the thought of being above human law.

'Wait', I thought, I am not dead yet and I vowed to make an impact on this world before I go. 'Yes' there is still time.

Rosie was standing outside the jeep, impatiently waiting for the procurement of this new dress, I walked over to her and threw my arms around her waist and swung her around until she was almost dizzy, as if to not risk her falling I pulled her in close to me and held her tightly for a brief moment. To say she was amazed was an understatement.

'Are you alright Mister Rogers? She blurted. 'Yes Rosie,' I said, 'never better, now it's time to go shopping' We stopped off at the grandest store we could find and not only did I buy her a dress, she got shoes and then a lovely silk scarf as well. She was almost crying with gratitude, but that only made me more extrovert, in my antics, I was swinging my arms all over the place, telling her that money did not matter, was there anything else she wanted, I shouted at the top of my voice.

'Today you are my Queen, the most important person in the world.'

The various counter staff looked on and must have thought that this man had just won the pools or lost his mind. I could not explain the emotion, but I knew it was bound to come 'down to earth with a bang' soon.

I recall seeing a policeman, putting a parking ticket on a car at a bus stop and I actually was tempted to just pull up and park, right beside him.

'What could he do? Send the fine, where? I can bet that no one knows the post codes for heaven or …hell.

Ironically, an extra highlight of Rosie's day was the fact that in my company none of the shop assistants in any of the shops, treated or indeed recognised her as a 'traveller.' Her satisfaction on this issue was not because of any shame but because she believed, she had found the ability to integrate.

I was really glad she was with me that day, as it dissipated some of the self-pity that would have been imminent in my mind. It seems strange even now looking back, that once the initial shock receded I actually looked forward to cramming in so much in the little time that I had been granted.

In fact, it is something every man realises, we all have to leave this life some day, but it is only a lucky few know exactly when. In addition, it is evident indeed that my time was going to be spent much differently.

This impending finality would be, a chance to say goodbye, a chance to say sorry and indeed a chance to be honest. I would now have a different attitude in my thoughts, deeds and actions. I have to live for today, as there will be no tomorrow. I knew that my time was now predefined and I was going to take my chances. Hope of longevity was now suddenly replaced with a desire to impact, although physically ill and weak, I felt, I was now more impenetrable and stronger than ever.

On the return trip from Limerick, Rosie, hugged the bags containing her new apparel, but about ten minutes before we reached Rahane, She asked, 'Can I put on my new clothes and shoes, I would love Mamma to see them?'

I nodded in the affirmative, but I actually doubt that, what ever my answer was, it was not going to influence her decision. She reached into the bag and held the new dress up to once again admire its beauty.

This time the disrobing procedure was more like an escapologist with a bag bound by chains. I am sure that at one stage both the old and the new dresses were totally inter tangled.

It was certain now that the lesson in modesty on our first encounter was well learned.

A big sigh of relief confirmed the completion and the old dress and shoes, were consigned to the shopping bag, and then dispatched to the rear seat of the jeep, never to see daylight again.

CHAPTER 28

It was nearing dusk and I was not in the perfect frame of mind to meet with Kathleen O' Donoghue, but I could not deny Rosie her moment of glory. Even if it meant the discussion on my medical state, probably resetting my depression.

When we reached the 'camp site', Rosie rushed out of the jeep, hardly allowing it to come to a stop. 'Look Mamma, what ya think?' She shouted as she fluttered like a dying wasp at a window. She ran around the fire, waving and gesturing to her young brothers.

'Look what mister Rogers bought for me?' Her mother stood up and watched in approval for a short while, and then she turned and looked directly at me with a gaze that I could not quite interpret. Was this I thought a stare of mistrust, cautiousness or joy. My feeble effort at a smile did not reciprocate any enlightenment either. So I just waited for her to speak and express her thoughts exactly, little did I realise how perceptive the woman was.

'Won't ya join us, Mister Rogers? Would ya like a spot of tea?' She asked, 'now that you has the bad news, to the back of your mind a little.'

She gestured to an old stool that had seen

many a rump.

'At times,' she continued. 'The man above gets greedy and wants all the good people with him and leaves the baddies on this earth.'

It may seem remarkable but my short acquaintance with Kathleen O' Donoghue, had led me to expect her to be as discerning as she was.

Little Jimmy did however cause one moment of embarrassment when he asked, 'Ma, why did Mister Rogers, buy all those things for Rosie?'

Kathleen replied, 'When the bold men came here the other night, Rosie's old dress got tore, so she had to get another. Now sstop axing questions.'

'But he continued, 'Rosie says Mister Rogers is her boyfriend, is he Ma?'

'She just replied in a matter of fact fashion, 'Mister Rogers is a friend to us all, a good friend, now be off and play. Will ya!'

He ran away from us but went directly over to Rosie who had by now calmed down a little. He looked at her and started singing, 'Rosie's got a boyfriend, Rosie's got a boyfriend.'

Then in mid song he stopped, as if hit by a bolt of lightening and walked slowly over to me and said, 'Mister Rogers, tamorra, is my birtday, I'm havin a party, will ya come down?'

Kathleen, immediately replied, 'I tink Mister Rogers has udder tings ta be doin dan comin to your party.'

'No I said,' I am invited, now so how can I refuse.'

He nodded his head at my acceptance and just turned, then disappeared through the hedgerow. Without any reaction to the comments of her brother, Rosie just walked over to her mother and me and placed a crumpled, shopping bag over an old tyre to prevent any dirt staining the new dress and she then sat down beside us. Her presence of course killed any further conversation about my illness, but I knew that no more needed to be said in any event. Kathleen looked at me and said.

'She has the same habit as her fadder, has ta be in on every conversation.'

I enquired as to the whereabouts of Willie. She told me that he had a couple of days work in the next village repairing a water tank.

'He rides dere everyday on the mare as tis too far ta walk. He should be home soon, but deres no need for me to get his tea as de farmers wife feeds him well.

Fact he brings home some of her home made bakin, 'tis gorgeous tho. Oh, if only Willie could get more work around here, we could stay maybe 'til springtime, but nobody in Rahane will give him work, certainly, now that he made enemies wit the school childer and dere parents.'

'I asked her what her plans were after Rahane and she said she could not wait for the school period to end to affect her immediate departure.

She further promised that she did not intend to ever return here.

'No, were not so badly off, we have friends near Dublin, called the Ryans.

We will stay with dem for the winter, 'tis a long time since we met dem, but we used ta know dem well one time.'

She winked at me and said, 'I thinks Rosie had a shine for little Tony, but dat id be telling tales.'

I could see Rosie was furious, but at least she had the discretion not to mention that we had already spoken of the Ryan's existence. As I glanced at her, I could sense a finger down the throat moment.

Even though it did not seem long, it had, by now become quite dark. Time must have moved quicker than I had thought.

I suggested to Kathleen, that it was time for me to leave the campsite and return to the cottage. As I got up to leave, I said thank you to her for her hospitality and said goodnight to everybody including Rosie. However, to my quite surprise, she got up and said goodbye to everyone as well.

She just automatically assumed she was staying again tonight at the cottage. I looked at her mother, and her mother just shrugged her shoulders, as a nod of approval.

We got into the jeep and drove the short

distance to the cottage, which was now completely in darkness. Just before we got out of the jeep, I said to Rosie.

'You know very shortly you will have to go back and stay with your parents and your brothers once again, I am certain that they all miss having you around.

It is not right', I continued, I had to choose my words carefully, 'For a young girl like you to be staying in a cottage alone with an older man like me.'

Immediately I saw her demeanour drooping and in an effort to try and cheer her up I said, 'Come on let's put on a big roaring fire and sit beside it, we will talk about things that you would like to do in the future.'

I thought this would cheer her up, but in fact, it seemed to make things worse.

She had treated the mention of returning home to the campsite almost as a mark of rejection.

I went into the cottage thinking that she would follow on, very shortly.

I immediately started racking up some kindling to light the fire. Every moment I expected her to come through the door, but there was no sign of her.

It was well into the evening, probably up to two hours later when I went out and she was still sitting in the jeep in a brooding state.

I sat into the driver's seat of the jeep, which was now, quite cold, and I said, 'Come on into cottage and we will talk about this.' To which she immediately replied, 'You don't like me do you?' I said, 'Of course I like you Rosie, now do not be so silly,' I tried to explain, 'it is not that, it is just a simple case of I am much older and…' I could have said that I was going to die very shortly, but that would have seemed like too good an excuse. I tried to give the indication that my life was short and whereas hers was long and if she lived it correctly, she would have many years of brightness and plenty of things to look forward to.

It was only when I put my hand on hers that she began to brighten up a little.

Then I said, 'Look Rosie if it is any consolation to you, I am telling you honestly that you are the only person that I really care for.

You see I do not have any family, I do not have brothers or sisters, and I do not have any kin living in London. I do not even have a dog, like old Frank.

You are the closest person to me; in fact, you are my best friend in this world. I would not do anything to harm my best friend, now would I?'

'Do you really mean that?'

'Yes of course, now come on in out of the cold.' I prompted.

She continued to clench my hand and jumped over the gear stick and followed me out the driver's side, rather than let go of my hand.

As we got to the door, once again she asked, 'Do you really care for me?'

When I answered in the affirmative, I actually saw a tear in her eye.

Eventually as children do, she started to brighten up a little bit and when the roaring fire was at it's maximum she went to the bedroom and took off her new dress and once again reappeared wearing my shirt.

I did not mind, in fact, I was quite chuffed, at the idea that she was again at ease wearing something that was so unbecoming of her fashion sense.

We sat by the fire and we spoke of many varied subjects, which included, her future, her schooling and even the Ryan family. The latter was spoken about because of her mother, revisiting the topic. Rosie was quite adamant that there was no way she was ever going to go stay with the Ryan's, or marry any of them.

'I just don't like them, and I don't see why I have to do what Mama and Dadda tell me, if I don't want to.'

I knew, however, that if that was the will of the travelling community, then, some day she would succumb to their wishes.

It was nice that at regular intervals, she would ask me about her new dress, looking for confirmation of her beauty, being complimented by the garment. One thing the news of my imminent demise was teaching me was that there was no more room, dishonesty, or vagueness. I will speak, as it is my last speech.

I said, 'Rosie, some day you will understand, that you possess a raw beauty that does not need a fancy dress to portray, you are as beautiful as beauty gets.'

She did not fully understand the sentiment but she did realise it was a compliment. A comfortable, silence descended and she lay her head against my leg like an adoring puppy.

Suddenly, she stood up abruptly as if startled by thunder, 'I nearly forgot, I have something for you, I have it in the room.'

She ran hastily to where she had disrobed and returned just as quickly, This time she was carrying a single plastic, red rose, I laughed within myself at the artificialness of the bloom, but it was as if she read my mind, when she said.

'Mister Rogers, My name is Rose, ...The flower that grows in a garden is a rose and this ...is a plastic rose...' 'The real rose only lasts for a season; this rose...will never wither.

So which do you think should be more like true friendship?'

I was stunned to hear the eloquence of her analysis.

'This is a gift from me to you, my best friend.'

As she presented it, she leaned forward and kissed me gently.

CHAPTER 29

Before I could analyse the moment further, there was a knock at the door, well more like a scratch on the door. I recognised it immediately as being the knock sign of old Frank, I leaned back in my chair and shouted, 'Frank, come on in.'

He walked in and he apologised for calling so late at night.

'Mister Rogers sir, I just want to tell you that them people were here twice looking for you.'

I said, "What people Frank, did you know them?'

He replied, 'Ah, yes, there was the priest, the teacher and another woman I had never seen before. They didn't hang about for long, they were looking for you.

The woman was wearin a suit, and she looked all official like.

They called two times, first, about two o' clock and again about half four.

They asked me, if I know where you were, and I told them I didn't, so they said they would be back again tomorrow.

I hope they don't mean trouble sir, looked like they were in for trouble.

'Ah no, it is all right Frank I can handle them. It is just the town people about the caravan at the gateway. They are still trying to get me to move it.'

'Oh be god', he quickly replied,' they've been trying to do that for years sir, Anyway, I'll be off now, if there's anything you need Sir, I'll call down again tomorrow.'

I replied, 'I'm okay Frank, I don't need anything, in fact tomorrow I might relax and go down by the river and do a spot of fishing.'

'Boy, I hope the day is as pleasant as you expect it to be sir,' he said as he turned and walked out the door.

When Frank left, Rosie asked me about Frank, who he was and how I knew him. I told her when we were living in London he was the caretaker.

'He lives on the hills just at the back of the house and from his front bedroom he can actually see down the meadow right down to this house. It was important when we were not here to know that someone was looking after it. In addition, he kept the grass cut; the hedges trimmed and even did a spot of painting while we were not here. Frank is a good old friend; he never let me down and was always there if I needed him.

He was a great servant to Margo's mum and her family while they were alive. Then he was a good servant to Margo and me until her death.

He got the house ready for me, before I left London and he has been a great help since my arrival here. I just wish there were more people like him. It was he, in fact who allowed your Dad and Mum to stay on the plot of land at the gate for the last four years before I came over here to live permanently. The one thing that you will notice about Frank is that he is never alone, if you step outside the door this minute as Frank walks away, I will guarantee you that you would see his old collie dog walking beside him.

Mo is the dog's name. I think if you look at Frank and then look at the dog, you will see that because they have been together so long they actually look like one and other.'

She started to laugh at this idea, but I continued.

'Frank has this long big sheepish looking beard exactly like Mo, and they share the same dark blue eye colour. I am sure they were born to be together; in fact, it is possible that the dog is almost as old as Frank, but without each other, I would say they would die within a week.'

'There you go then,' she proclaimed, 'Frank has 'Mo', and you have me.'

The content of that sentence, was too much for me to analyse at that moment.

At least now, she was back to pleasant mood again. Quite a transformation from an hour ago, when she sat, brooding in the jeep.

Therefore, I knew it was acceptable to suggest.

'I think its time for you to head to bed Miss and I will see you in the morning.'

Reluctantly she got up, reached over kissed me on the cheek and went off to bed.

I for my part got some old blankets from the press, the ones I had been using for the last few days, and I pulled the old couch up near the fire and went off to sleep.

The cottage did have a second bedroom, but it had not been used for quite some time and dampness was rife, besides it would be a shame to let a roaring open fire project it self into an empty room.

As I started to drift off to sleep, the pain on my side reminded me of my short future. It did help to take a few sips from the *potion of sustenance*.

'What a day', I thought, 'as for tomorrow, and my immanent visitation of the 'witch of gloom', and her deputation from the village.'

I had made up my mind, at that point, that if she were to ask me once more about moving the O' Donoghue family, then I would personally dump her in the 'Sprid.'

What can they do to me?

Absolutely nothing, oh the satisfaction', I thought.

'Bring on tomorrow.'

CHAPTER 30

The following morning I got up quite late. But to my surprise, there was still no movement from the bedroom. I lit the fire and started to cook the breakfast; I thought that the aroma from the food would at least wake her up and bring her out of hibernation.

It was not too long though when another interruption caused me a lot more distress.

Old Frank had warned me, the night before that a deputation was on its way, but I had never expected them to arrive so early, yes there they were all in force standing at the front door.

The viper Francis, Father Turley, and this time a very tall, slender looking lady, looking exactly as Frank had described, dressed in a very pale suit, something you were more likely to wear to a wedding or funeral than to meet somebody on their doorstep.

She had a folder in her hand; the contents really aroused my curiosity. I am sure these folders made her feel and seem official.

She was a tall gentle looking, woman. Her red- hair peeped out from a type of scarf like headgear that she wore.

She said, 'Mister Rogers, I am Sister O' Brien from the Daughter's of charity, social services in Limerick, the child welfare section.

I have come to investigate the welfare of a young lady called Rosie O' Donoghue.'

I had never come face to face with a nun before, but somehow genuineness seemed to radiate from her eyes.

As she referred to her notes, she asked, 'Do you know this girl?'

I said, 'Of course I do, her family are friends of mine. Good friends of mine, I stressed.'

I went on to tell her what she probably already knew, but somehow, I thought that when talking to her she was assessing my persona.

She is the daughter of the people who are staying… 'She did not let me finish, but interrupted in a mild calming tone, 'and where is she now?'

I replied, 'She is asleep in her bed.'

To which the viper Francis added, 'You mean in your bed, isn't that right Mister Rogers,' I told you didn't I, I knew if we came here early, we would catch them,' she said gleefully as she looked directly at the nun.

'No it's not at all like that,' I replied defensively.

'Well then what is it like? Mister Rogers, The Viper interjected.

I focused my entire gaze at the sister, firstly, in an effort to confirm my innocence and secondly because I believed, she was truly listening and acting without any preconceptions.

'Young Rosie has had a harrowing ordeal of being attacked by some drunken louts and had it not been for her own quick thinking, she would be in a very serious physical and emotional state.

Her mother asked me to accommodate her in the cottage here to give her a little more comfort than having her recover in a cramped, gypsy caravan.

It was a more convenient location also, to facilitate the Doctor to treat her in privacy.'

I noticed the nun, nodding in approval of my argument, so I used this affirmation to direct my next statement at 'the viper'.

'As a matter of fact, yes, she is in my bed… but if you look near the fire, you will see that is where I slept, her mother had no reservation,' I attempted to continue, but the Viper spoke over me. 'Her mother, her mother, ! She fumed, her mother would not recognise danger if it bit her in the leg.' she continued, 'That woman, has an I.Q. of a rubber boot, all she could see, was someplace to dump her kid and let someone else look after them for free.'

I was incensed but for Rosie's sake, I could not show my anger.

'Look I have had enough of this, Sister, what exactly do you want?' I asked.

However, before she answered Father Turley, who, until now was waiting quietly in the wings, spoke out.

'Look John, we are both men of the world and you must understand that it looks wrong, for a young innocent girl to be staying in a house with an elderly man, like yourself, and you devoid of the company of a woman this long time.

'Father', I said, 'With all due respect can I put a question to you?

If I were to subscribe to your theology for a moment and acknowledge that there is a superior being up there waiting to assess me on my judgement day.

Would he condemn me for seeking the joy of a young persons company, in my life?

On the other hand, indeed condemn the young lady for seeking stimulating, conversational enlightenment?

Does any of this fall under what you're religion would term a sin?

He was slow to answer and when he did, it was devoid of any great conviction.

'I suppose, the good Lord, would be able to see into your mind and assess your true motivation, and assuming your thoughts were pure than of course there would be no sin committed.'

'Well then,' I immediately replied, 'If your God exonerates me, but then You, Miss Francis and the people of Rahane do not, are you then declaring that you lot, have more wisdom than your God?'

His response was one of defensiveness, but I am sure it was intended to sway the opinion of the Social worker.

'Well, from what Miss Francis has reported to me, we are not sure as to your true motivation and that is the reason, why, we are here today.

Nothing may have happened yet, but, is it not better to remove the temptation than risk pending harm?'

Immediately sensing my rising anger, the nun intervened.

'Mister Rogers, will you promise me that you will return this young lady to her parents today and I will call again to visit her, later on in the week and assess her welfare in her home environment and I am sure we will not need to meet again?'

I knew better than to offer resistance and reluctantly agreed.

'Right,' she continued, ' We will be off then, as we have no further business here.'

Miss Francis looked at her in amazement as if I was given a reprieve from the death sentence. I could still here, her objecting to the soft approach adopted by the nun as they walked down the drive.

I went back into the house, feeling that I had won some sort of a moral victory over Francis and Turley.

I did appreciate the wisdom of the nun however, it was obvious that she had encountered many a domestic situation and I suppose she was a little like Coskin in ways, in that she adopted, a 'knock before the Jack boot strategy', which only comes with experience and the ability of having no fixed agenda prior to conflict.

I put on the kettle and started making the breakfast. Right on, cue, as the kettle boiled, my young companion emerged from the bedroom. 'Morning, Mister Rogers, as she came over and gave me a 'peck' on the cheek.'

'Good job' I thought, 'that the viper did not witness that.'

'You are in good spirits this morning. What's the occasion?' I enquired.

'Today, don't you remember?' she said 'Its Jimmy's birthday and I am going to the caravan to help Mamma bake some nice food, then I am going to come back here, then I am going to have a bath and wash my hair and then I'm going to put on my new dress for the party.'

Her exuberance brought back memories, of the time now long gone, when I was back in London and meeting Margo for the first time.

'I must get some pennies from Dadda, to buy him some sweets, what are you getting him as a present?'

'My god', I thought, 'a present, I will have to go down to the village and see what I can find.'

I knew right then, that my plans for a days fishing were well and truly scuppered.

Rosie accompanied me as far as the campsite, and I then went alone to the village to buy a present for Jimmy. I knew that my purchase of the dress for Rosie was the main reason, that he had invited me to his party. He knew that I would not attend the function with 'my hands hanging.'

The only place in the village likely to have any thing suitable was Foley's so I headed straight there.

Rachel Foley was the only person I saw on entering the shop because my eyes took time to adjust to the contrast between natural and artificial light. She greeted me with a pleasant smile and enquired as to my well-being.

She continued, 'Is it the bread and milk, I'll be getting ya?' As this was my customary order.

'No' I replied, 'I am looking for a toy for a little lad's birthday, can you suggest anything?'

'If you give me a minute, I will go to the store room and see if there is anything that is suitable.'

As I waited by the counter, I could now see clearly in the pale light, and to my horror I saw Josie O' Leary, sitting in the corner, with his two accomplices. I thought to myself please let's not have any confrontation, I was just not in the mood right now. Young Rachel returned with a small-boxed, toy truck.

'This is all we have I am sorry.' I looked at it and said, 'No, well done this is perfect, and if you have a birthday card, I'll be on my way.'

'Well well, there's no end to your talent is there Mister Rogers?' Said a voice moving quickly towards me from behind.

I should have ignored the question, as I knew it was from Josie O' Leary, but stupidly I asked for clarification.

'It doesn't seem to matter to you whether its little girls or little boys you play with, does it now?' Before I could react the taller of the other men, Peadar Scanlon, came forward quite abruptly and put both his hands on O' Leary's shoulders and steered him away to where they had been sitting, 'Come on now Josie, that's enough, Look forget about him and enjoy your drink.' He instructed.

I was quite surprised at the action of Scanlon and indeed quite grateful. I did think it strange at the time as to why he did not support O'Leary, rather than restrain him.

Rachel wrapped the gift and as she did so, she uttered an apology under her breath. 'O' Leary was not finished however, because as I neared the exit he shouted out, 'It's only a matter of time Rogers, before you will be forced to leave Rahane. There's no place for you English bastards here, nor indeed the likes of them tinkers, you do be hanging around with, nothing a match and a bottle of kerosene wouldn't solve, get out I tell ya, get out!'

I was indeed glad to have left the shop, but I could not help wondering, how shallow his life was to be in a pub drinking at such an early time of the day.

CHAPTER 31

As I reached the gates of the cottage, I could not believe the transformation that had been carried out in my short time to the village. The camp was now enclosed in a circle of homemade ribbons, strings and buntings, a make shift gazebo had been erected using a piece of tent material and the most noticeable attraction was the fabulous aroma of a barbecue.

Willie immediately invited me to join him for a drink, but I knew by the expression on Kathleen's face that Willie was in fact attempting to use me as an alibi for his excuse to drink and possibly while so doing, was avoiding some chore or other.

I declined by saying I had to get a few hours rest, in anticipation of the vigorous night that lay ahead.

Before leaving, I complimented them both on the wonderful effort; they had put into the preparation and told them, that I was looking forward to the event. Kathleen expressed a doubt about the inclemency of the weather and attempted to justify the gazebo.

Willie interjected, 'Tis always the same wit dat woman, she spects de worst in everyting, a fool can see dat dere will be no rain, taday.' No sooner were the words out of his mouth than rain drops descended on the camp.

'You're a witch I tell ya, a witch' as he sheepishly looked at his wife with a defeated smile.

'Men ya tinks ya knows it all', I knew she could not help but put the poor man, in his place.

She then turned her attention to me and said, 'As ya see de 'princess' is already gone ta your house, ta get herself dolled up, I tink she is looking forward to de night more dan de boys.'

She went on to tell me that Willie had completed the job on the water tank and as an extra token of appreciation the farmer gave him a small pig to roast for the party.

I could not help thinking as I walked towards the cottage that even for all Willie's strength, he was no match for his partner and he should have realised his inferiority by now.

'You don't have to be strong to rule.'

Looking back, I played the same role with Margo, so I cannot talk.

Since Margo's death, however I was my own man. Not answerable to any woman. I opened the door of the cottage and I met Rosie, flitting from the bedroom to the bathroom, she looked at me and said, 'Well it took you a long time to go to the village.' I knew her comment was in jest, but made me think all the same as to women's hierarchical position in the universe. I smiled as I could hear her singing in the bathroom.

I shouted a brief, 'Will you be long?'

She responded. 'Just doing my hair, be out in a jiff.'

I looked at the clock over the fireplace and deduced that it was at least another, four hours before the party. I was fascinated by her enthusiasm in preparing so prematurely.

I stroked up the fire and decided to let her do her own thing all I wanted to do was relax and sleep for a while as the morning had indeed been both eventful and stressful.

In my present circumstances, when faced with aggression I noticed a decrease in my state of health.

It was not long indeed, before I drifted off to sleep, I had a strange dream involving Margo and Rosie together, where Margo was taking the same stance as the villagers and objecting to my friendship with the young lady. She was standing by an open window, threatening to push Rosie to her death. She was shouting at me to choose between them.

'It's either her or me, you can't have us both.'

I found myself saying, 'It has to be Rosie.'

She stomped her foot in anger and said, 'Well if it's not me then it's nobody.'

She immediately caught Rosie by the hair and slung her out the window. I reached out to try to save her and shouted her name.

It was then that Rosie shook me to an awaking state, 'You alright? You were calling my name. Were you dreaming about me?'

I was quite embarrassed, as I blurted, 'How long have I been asleep?'

'About three hours', she replied, 'I was going to wake you soon anyway, just after I finish with my hair.'

'Finish with your hair!' I joked. 'You tell me I have been asleep for three hours, yet as I was drifting asleep I reckon you were starting to do your hair.

This must be the longest hair do in history.'

Then as my eyes focused on her I saw she was still wearing only a bath towel. I knew better than to ask aloud but what in the blazes has she being doing for three hours. Nevertheless, I suppose that is a woman's privilege.

I smiled to myself, thinking if it took Rosie a few hours to make herself pretty, than how long it would take Miss Francis.

Rosie could measure her time with a clock; the latter would have to use a calendar.

CHAPTER 32

I eventually forced myself to get off the couch, the lure of the blazing fire and the comfortable blanket, made the 'task' even less appealing.

I trudged to the bathroom, with the dream still in my head. Was Margo I wondered trying to tell me something? Was she indicating that Rosie had to leave? Was it my conscious telling me that I would have to lose my friend? How was I going to tell her about the commitment I gave to the nun, earlier that day? What about the commitment I have given to Rosie? I have to tell her tonight, but when? Perhaps if the party is a success, she might realise that her place is with her family. What ever happens I do not want to lose her out of my life.

After a quick shave, I went into the bedroom, to find a clean shirt, but what confronted me is a sight I was never to forget.

Standing in front of me was a young girl, who had just become a lady. She had anticipated my coming in to the room, and had perfected a statuesque, pose to highlight her beautiful features. She was now fully made up, complete with the new dress and scarf, her hair was glistening in the faded light and the new shoes completed the revelation. She looked every part a woman, in a way it was sad to see the child replaced by such elegance, but on the other hand, it was exhilarating to see the transformation.

She reminded me for a moment of a doll in a trinket box. Had I taken an hour to view her appearance, then she would have held that pose for that time.

'Rosie, you look so beautiful', I was genuine in my praise, ' I have never seen any woman, prettier than you, just wait until your family see you.'

I was equally amazed by the joy at my words of vindication, as she probed for more.

'Do you really think I look pretty?' She continued, 'I don't care what my family think; it's what you think is all that matters to me.'

I felt my eyes swelling to a tear, but best not to show it. It was a fantastic feeling to be able to bring such joy to another human, just by the purchase of a simple dress.

As I put on a shirt and jacket she must have jumped around the room, one hundred times, such was her delight.

When she knew I was ready to leave, she linked my arm and we walked together towards the front door.

'Oh, wait,' I said, 'if you open the press by the sink, you will see the little gift I got for Jimmy', as I gestured to her to walk back across the room. However, instead of letting go my arm, she dragged me as well towards the unit. Eventually, with all our shackles intact we headed down the lane to the camp.

As we walked, I was not in any way embarrassed to have Rosie by my side in such fashion; in fact, I was so proud that she was there.

In addition, when her parents looked and saw their 'princess', I bet they did not even see me.

They both walked towards her as if she been away for ten years. Willie found it difficult to show emotion, but what he lacked Kathleen, showed in abundance.

'Oh Rosie', she blurted, 'your like one of dem, women from the pictures… A proper film star, oh, and Mister Rogers, tis fine yure looking as well.'

'Come on in, and shtop nattering,' Willie, insisted. 'What ill it be Mister Rogers?

As he gestured with an upward movement of his half clenched fist.'

'Whatever you have Willie, I like a little 'toddy', if you have one.'

'Comin roite up sir.' He said as he tried to imitate my English accent.

'Now' I enquired 'Where is the birthday boy?'

As if summoned from a far, Danny came running through the hedge, he stopped and announced his brother. He moved both arms to the same side, like a courtier announcing a prince and said, 'Here he is Mister Rogers, Jimmy O' Donoghue.'

Jimmy ran to where I was now seated as he waited for his inevitable prize.

'Here you are young man; I hope you have many happy hours playing with it.'

So much, I thought for young Rachel Foley's neat parcelling, as the wrapper gave no resistance to the vulture like peeling of the little hands, 'Oh its, bril, Mister Rogers, just bril. Come on Danny, let's build a garage in the sand,' as they disappeared as quickly as they had come.

As they exited, they could be heard making the sound of a big truck, pulling logs, with the obligatory sound of the air brakes as they turned around the corner.

'Tis a good job, I put up the canvas', Willie said, 'Cause here comes the rain. I knew all along it would rain.'

'Well ya fibber Willie O' Donoghue, you said ezacly de opposite' Kathleen replied.

I do not think any of us however realised how torrential the rain was to be, because after fifteen minutes, it had turned the ground into a swamp and as for the fire, it was now a whimpering bunch of cackling embers. Everyone including the half-roasted pig was sheltering, under the canvas that was now beginning to show its true age.

As the water lodged on the roof, its sheer weight started to find weaknesses in the fabric.

It was only a matter of time before it too would succumb to the more powerful forces of nature.

Little Jimmy, was obviously the most upset of all as he felt that the forces of nature had ganged up on him to ruin his 'big day'.

'On normal days like dis,' Kathleen said, 'We would all get in the wagon, til de rain sstoped, but tis the pig I'm worried about.'

Rosie immediately offered a suggestion, which was in content very practical, but in misconception, very flawed.

'I know let's all go up to our house, sure the fire is still lighting and tis warm and cosy.' she suggested.

Kathleen and I exchanged a wry smile and all I could say was, 'Yes why not, it won't take long to move everything if I bring down the jeep.'

But Willie had a better idea, he suggested just lifting the barbecue into the back of the Gypsy wagon, and in two minutes he could have it hitched up, then there would be no need for anyone to get wet.

'Specially da drink, as dats already in the wagon.' He laughed at his own self-perceived cleverness. To be fair to Willie he was a man of his word, because that is approximately all the time it took. In less than five minutes we were all on our way, on the short journey to 'our' cottage.

Willie left the wagon hitched and he tied the horse to a small fence, near the back door.

Ten minutes later, we were installed in the living room as if we had been there all day.

Jimmy and Danny were once again, 'half way around the globe' with their haulage business.

Willie was lounging in the armchair, with very little liquid left in a large brown bottle.

Kathleen was basting the pig, which was now suspended across two jagged bricks from the hearth, and Rosie was standing in front of the mirror, running her fingers through her hair, with a broad smile of total pride in her appearance.

I for my part just sat by the table and drew immense satisfaction from the knowledge that I was making a difference to these people's lives.

After a short while, Kathleen announced that the meal was ready, and all had generous portions. Danny was an immense help to her, both in the distribution of the meals and laterally in the dispatch of the ware to the sink.

Willie and Rosie seemed to take the view that, these chores did not concern them. I assumed that Willie was showing me his dominant position.

In Rosie's case, it was because the slightest spillage would blemish or stain the perfection that she was so eager to protect. When cleanliness was restored, we all formed a semi-circle, around the fireplace. Rosie pushed Jimmy away from a position he had taken by my side. The altercation went almost, unnoticed, as Jimmy knew better than to confront Rosie when she was in her possessive mode. A slight shirk of his shoulder was his total resistance.

Kathleen quickly intervened as only she knew how and firstly led everyone in a dedication to Jimmy, culminating in the 'Happy birthday' song.

Rosie, immediately prompted her mother to sing a song, 'Mister Rogers, never heard you singing Ma, go on.'

I looked towards Kathleen and she nodded a confirmation without any further persuasion.

'Id like ta sing a song dats made famous by a traveller girl, or as we say a *Pavee Lackeen,* she is originally from county Cork and her name is Margaret Barry. De song is called *She moved tro' de fair.'*

I watched as she lifted her head out of her shoulders and gently closed her eyes. She descended into a world of uninterrupted passion, it was as if everything around had now stood still, simply to allow her complete the aria. Everybody in the room even the little baby seemed to stare in amazement, transfixed by the enchanting rendition.

Even after she had finished, a silence encapsulated a lapse in time to allow the reverberation of the melody to gently drift into obscurity. A combined cheer and a round of applause of course followed this. The impact for me was so intense, that even thinking of the song now invokes a haunting, eerie image in my mind.

After a while, Willie walked towards the fireplace and looked, endearingly at the gun that hung above. To satisfy his curiosity, I suggested he examine it more closely, I told him it belonged to Margo's father but that I knew little else of its history. I did say however, that Coskin had mentioned about the abundance of them in Irish homes around the 'rebel' counties.

Willie took it in his hands as if he had handled many a similar weapon before.

'Coskin is right.' He said.

He went on to explain that this is known as a 'fenian' gun, it was used by rebel Irish freedom fighters, in their fight against 'the black and tans' an elite, British army unit who 'took no prisoners'.

He went on to mention that most of the guns used by the Irish Freedom fighters, were in fact captured or stolen from the British. He showed me where a plate had been removed, which was evident by the broken rivet marks.

That plate he informed me was where the English badge was located.

They are properly called 303s, as this was the bore of the gun. The guns themselves were generally in poor condition as they had been in service for decades.

Willie's familiarisation with the weapon was one of a maintenance nature, where he had seen his father restoring them to make them an item of pride to display in the same fashion as this one.

He said they were primarily meant as a statement of freedom but also he added as a safeguard in case, 'The English came again.'

It was only after uttering this quote did he realise what he had just said. Kathleen looked up to the roof in embarrassment at his lack of tact. I only laughed it off as a joke, knowing that he had meant no malice whatever.

'This one,' he continued, 'is in lovely 'nick' and never seen any repair.'

I gestured to him to reach to the top shelf in the cabinet, as it was here a box of shells, were stored that I assumed fitted the weapon.

He immediately took down the unopened box of bullets, sat down by the table, and inserted five shells into the magazine. Kathleen shouted at him to take the bullets out, as it was likely to 'go off and kill someone.'

He ignored her objection and I did not seem concerned on this occasion because I recognised his confident handling and his experienced familiarity.

The gun suddenly ceased to be a matter of conversation as the now familiar 'scratch' on the door interrupted us, which announced the arrival of old Frank.

I called to him, to come in and I complimented his sense of timing, 'You can smell the free drink a mile away, I joked.

'Will you join us for a drop?'

He immediately declined, 'No thanks, just want to take old Mo for a stroll down the village, while the rain stays away for a spell. But it looks like I am just in time to save someone from being shot' he joked, as he looked at Willie holding the rifle.

He continued, 'I really called to check in to see if you got on alright with the town council, this morning.'

'Everything fine', I replied, very dismissively.

'Just dat when de priest and de teacher are tageter, it means trouble for someone.'

My attempt to make little of the query, only succeeded in highlighting it, because as soon as Frank had left; Kathleen proceeded to quiz me further.

'You are in trouble cause of us Mister Rogers, aren't you?' She asked.

I felt no reason to lie and even if I did, I knew Kathleen O' Donoghue, would see right through it.

'Just that Miss Francis contacted the Daughters of Charity, to investigate her complaint about young Rosie staying with me here at the cottage.'

Willie immediately sat up from his slouched position and one could see the fire in his eyes, as he started to get mad. Worse than that, he gestured with a loaded gun.

'Dat bloody bitch, she wont be happy till

were all figten among one another. And the priest sure he's not much better.'

Kathleen interrupted, 'Willie O' Donoghue, how many times have I told ya about your language in front of the childer? And for God's sake put away dat gun.'

We all waited until he had in fact calmed down and sat back on the chair.

'Well anyway', I then continued, 'The nun asked me, to insure that Rosie would return immediately, to live with you and that she would look in on her during the week.'

Rosie immediately, turned to me and asked, 'What did you say to her?'

As she spoke, I saw immediately the reciprocal look in her eyes that I had just seen in her fathers.

Kathleen spared me the responsibility of telling her of my answer, by saying.

'Look Rosie, we don't want any more trouble for Mister Rogers, he has been more dan good to us and its not like were goin miles away, in fact if Mister Rogers will allow us, we will stay 'til after Christmas, What do ya say to dat?'

Rosie stood up in such a rage and marched towards the door, as she reached for the handle, she roared out a tirade of accusations that although I understood, I certainly did not expect.

She singled me out with her stare and with a look of defeat, she shouted.

'All you settled people are the same, the town hates me, the school hates me and now the only settled person I ever liked hates me as well. Well I hope you are happy now, you lied to me all this time, you promised I could stay here. Well now I hope you got your way. You know what? I hate you as well!'

She left, leaving the cottage shaking with the force of the slamming door.

Both her parents, by this time were on their feet and then the baby started to cry. Her mother tried to reassure me that this was the other side of Rosie, but she will calm down and come back in, in a moment. I however was a little more sceptical of a speedy, turnaround, when I considered the previous nights 'stand off' in the jeep.

I walked to the door with a heavy heart, thinking, 'Where is this Johnny Rogers, the person, who was ready to fight the world?'

I knew, that although the authorities could not touch me for not conforming to the nun's request it could however, spell separation for Rosie, from her family. I further realised that I would not be there to pick up the pieces.

I opened the door and walked to the wagon, where she had now taken residence.

'Rosie,' I whispered.

'Go away!' Was the instant reply 'I don't want to talk to you no more.'

As I stood at the end of the wagon, talking to the darkness, I was quite startled by this cloth like object that hit me in the face.

'You can have your stupid dress', she said, 'maybe, you'll find somebody else to give it to and tell them the same lies as you told me.'

I knew, at this point it was fruitless to argue, so I made as dignified a retreat as possible. Kathleen met me as I returned indoors; she took the dress from my hands and tried to console me by accusing Rosie of being a spoiled little brat, whom she mentioned was not beyond a birch.

I had no answer, to what had happened and I made an excuse to go to the bathroom, but I just needed time alone to calculate the best course of appeasement. I poured some water on my face as I looked, through tear-stained eyes, at this sorry excuse for a man.

'How,' I thought, 'could I do this to the most genuine person I had ever met. What life skill was this episode going to teach her, other than to be more mis-trusting of people, than she had ever been?'

CHAPTER 33

The next half hour of my life was the most defining time that anyone could ever experience.

If it were possible to delete any period in my sixty plus years than this was it.

The rain had once again started and it was not long before it was pounding on the window of the bathroom. I hoped Rosie would have some blanket or rug to keep her warm. Then through the din, I heard a male voice utter a monosyllabically shout.

'It must be old Frank', I deduced, 'He must be taking shelter from the rain and calling Mo to his side.

On returning to the living room, we were all startled by a shriek from outside, which was most definitely Rosie's voice. We ran in unison to the front door, just in time to see the horse drawn wagon careering down the drive. I saw Rosie appear in the dark standing at the back, shouting, 'Stop it, somebody, stop it!'

Already it had gone too far for any of us to help. Nevertheless, even if somebody had been coming the other way, stopping it would have been a risky manoeuvre.

The wagon had built up a momentum that

was now beyond the control of the mare. We all ran in pursuit at varying degrees of speed, hoping somehow that it would come to a miraculous stop.

Then if things could not get any worse, the startled and confused animal, veered off the lane and instead of heading towards the gate, she turned towards the embankment, which leads down to the Sprid.

In one fleeting moment, it had now disappeared out of sight and our worse fears were realised, when we heard a loud, crashing sound, followed by a morbid silence.

I shouted to young Danny, 'Go to my jeep and get the flash lamp from the glove compartment.'

Willie reached the wreckage, before me, but as I joined him, neither of us could make any sense of the scene.

We both kept calling out to Rosie, but all we could here in reply was the sporadic, heavy breathing of the mare. We quickly realised that she was badly injured and lying on her side.

We eventually found the back end of the wagon, which we could feel was partially submerged in the river.

No matter how we reached and poked in the dark, we could not find any sign of Rosie.

By now, I could see Danny, running down the embankment with the lamp, so I ran to meet him. I knew at this stage that every moment was vital.

When I returned to the scene, I can only say it was one of total horror; it was more like a combined wreckage of many wagons, as there were so many pieces strewn around.

I shone the lamp into, under and over the wagon, without revealing any sign of life. I shone it down at the poor mare just in time to see her give up her will to live. A combination of stress and injury had quickly taken its toll.

I had hoped that the mare was not the only life lost at the sprid that night. I shone the torch once more in despair at the turbulent river and there stuck in a fallen tree stump, lying face down in the river, was my princess.

I did not care how deep it was I had to expend any hope that she was still alive. I threw off my jacket and lay it with the lamp as I slid down the riverbank. Willie immediately, picked up the discarded torch and lit the scene.

By this time, Kathleen was now by his side holding on to him with sheer trepidation.

In the light, I could clearly see the horror. Her petit body frame, wrapped in the scant undergarment that had now become almost transparent by the water. Her hair that had taken an age to perfect was now a tangled mess draping over her head, floating on the mire.

I spun her around in my arms but she just drooped in total limpness. I was no medic, but I recognised from my early days as a butcher, when a body was lifeless.

On my way up to her parents, I picked up

my jacket and covered her modesty. Kathleen already recognised her morbid state, but Willie kept urging me to get her to a doctor as quick as possible.

He became so incessant in his demand that Kathleen had to slap him across the face with her open hand and said the words that still cut me to this day.

'Rosie, is dead Willie, our little angel is gone.'

At this point, I thought that she was a little cold in her portrayal of grief, but then Kathleen O' Donoghue, was such a complex character.

Willie on the other hand just took her in his arms and cried, inconsolably.

Jimmy and Danny just looked on, devoid of any comprehension as to what at just happened.

I for my part just could not believe the finality of the moment.

A few hours ago, she was linking my arm, with the vigour of a kitten with a ball of wool, now she was lifeless. Her smile, her beauty and her silliness, gone forever. Willie and Kathleen brought her back to the house and I agreed to go to the police station, to see if Coskin was about.

I got as far as the gate, where the wagon had been originally parked. I looked at the strewn litter that was destroyed by the rain. I stopped for a moment and looked pensively at the site, my heart got so heavy I could not move. I glanced over my shoulder, to discover the old discarded dress that she had changed out of on our return from Limerick. I reached over and picked it up, but as soon as I did, all kinds of imagery ran through my mind, and I then spontaneously exploded in convulsive crying.

Through the tears, I kept calling her name as if she would mystically reappear.

I then slumped over the steering wheel, with my head buried in the dress, all my emotions raced uncontrollably, my mind was in a haze and I found myself, crying repeatedly, 'I am sorry Rosie, so, so sorry.'

CHAPTER 34

I cannot even attempt to calculate how long I had been there, but I was shocked back to reality by the opening of the passenger door and the subsequent illumination of the interior light.

'You all right, Sir?' Was the worried tone of the speaker.

I looked through my swollen eyes, with a slightly embarrassed look to see old Frank, staring back at me.

'Yeah, yes I'm just shocked that's all.' I said. 'It is a lot to take in, it just happened so fast...'

'What happened so fast?' Was his instant query. 'The crash, the crash!,' I said quite accusative. 'You shouting out to Mo, must have startled the horse.'

'Me? What are you talking about?' He said. 'I am just on my way back from the village. Tell me what happened, for heaven's sake.'

I realised that he, genuinely knew nothing, nor was he in any way responsible.

He too sat for a moment in silence, after I related the events, but his pensiveness was quickly broken by an observation he made, which made events of the night even more sinister.

'As I was just leaving the village, a car almost knocked me down travelling at a ridiculous speed coming from this direction.

I got an awful fright because at first I thought it was a motor bike,' he said, 'because it only had one working headlight. The left hand light was out, so it was in fact much closer to me than I had realised. I had to jump onto the ditch to save myself.'

'A car?' I thought, 'surely we would have heard a car, if one had been at the cottage.'

Then I deduced that maybe with all the panic and noise we did not take any notice of a third party.

It was then the shocking realisation set in, I was certain I had heard a voice.

'Suppose,' I thought, 'that this person, released the reins from the gate and the voice was intended to startle the mare, which would mean that the stampede was started deliberately.

Then, if this was not an accident, it was murder.'

I gestured to Frank to put Mo in the back of the jeep and we all headed to the village to find Coskin. As there was no light at the police station, I went into the pub. The place was reasonably full with patrons and there seemed to be a jovial atmosphere. My entry did not seem to cause any great concern. I looked around and quickly took stock of all familiar faces, and this included Peadar Scanlon and the other man that was with Josie O' Leary, earlier that morning.

O' Leary however was not anywhere to be seen. I quickly found Coskin amongst a group over by the old piano; he was in his civvies, sporting an Arran sweater.

It did not take him long to ingest my briefing. He then quickly, went behind the bar of the pub to use the private phone to contact, Father Turley and Doctor Howard and to request their attendance at the cottage.

He travelled with us to the cottage, to avoid any delay.

On the way he quizzed Frank further as to the incident with the one head lighted car and he felt certain that its occupants were someway involved. Frank seemed quite vague about the make or model of the car, but he did seem certain, that there was only one person in the vehicle.

When we got to the cottage, the atmosphere was indeed one of gloom and despair. Everybody was wailing, including Kathleen and the two boys.

Rosie was now lying on the bed, lightly groomed and wearing her new dress once again. Although it looked inappropriate, I took the plastic rose that she had given to me and I placed it between her clasped fingers.

Father Turley did show a more caring side than I had ever witnessed from him as he led the congregation in a 'decade of the rosary'. He then anointed her with some oil and spoke softly to her as if in a secret conversation. It did strike me as a little shallow to hear him calling her 'My child'.

Coskin called on me to show him the wreckage of the wagon and the exact location of the body.

Just as we were leaving, a car pulled up to the cottage, driven by Miss Francis. I told her that she was not welcome but I had failed to notice, that she was transporting the Doctor.

Coskin also insisted that she remain in the car and that she was not to set foot inside the cottage. Despite her indignation, she knew that this was not the right time to meet Willie O' Donoughue.

Coskin viewed the accident site, extensively. He did not seem to find any clues as to its cause.

He did confirm that having spoken to Willie, he was certain that the reins of the horse had been physically tampered with. This belief was based on the theory that securing horses and realising their frisky nature would have been a skill that Willie would have perfected as a youth.

He then asked me, 'Would you drive me to the village and wait for me?'

I agreed to the request and en route he discussed his theory.

'The night of the first attack, that is the night Josie O' Leary was maimed. You may recall a car nearly ran us down leaving the Doctor's house.

Well on that night, that car too had only one headlamp. I knew that car to belong to Peadar Scanlon. It is very coincidental that a car with a similar defect was rushing from the scene tonight.

Therefore, Mister Scanlon is the starting point for my investigation.'

I thought it prudent to make one contra observation.

'When I fetched you at Foley's, I saw Peadar Scanlon drinking in the corner. I got the impression he had been there for some time, he did not look as if he had just arrived.'

We stopped outside Foley's and Coskin went into speak with Mister Scanlon. He returned in a very short time and said, 'We have a little drive to make, to the home of Josie O' Leary.'

It turned out that earlier that day, O' Leary had been with Scanlon and company, but said he had to go home to treat some sick animal on his little holding, so he took Scanlon's car.

'Rachel Foley,' he continued, 'confirmed your observation about Scanlon. He has not moved from his seat since early morning.'

'After all there is no competition, on a wet day between sitting by the fire in Foley's and building stonewalls in the rain.'

I have never hated anyone but my levels of tolerance had at this time plummeted to an all time low. I had yet to be convinced that O' Leary was not the culprit. In my mind, I had him convicted and sentenced already.

I contemplated, that if I ever knew for certain of his guilt, I would not be able to control my actions. 'Clearly,' I thought, 'if this is the case then, this man should never see freedom again.'

The route to his house took a strange meandering, bog like route and I was glad given all the rain, that we had taken the jeep.

The house itself was separated from the public road by a crescent shaped path that led past three other houses, finally arriving at a two-story building at the end.

Even in the poor light it struck me that the planning officer that sanctioned this mis-match of buildings was either blind or suffering some substance abuse because none of the buildings shared any common esthetical harmony.

The larger one, Coskin informed me, was the one that belonged to Josie O' Leary and family.

The entrance to the house was strewn with old cars, bicycles and a vast array of rusted farm machinery. There was a bright yard light, which illuminated the front of the building. I counted four dogs with different degrees of malnutrition, running around the yard barking as if, they had been beaten for hours.

Coskin got out of the jeep and walked straight over to a Ford Capri, that sat parked on what was once a flowerbed. The car was open and he reached in and turned on the lights, he walked to the front of the car and it clearly could be seen, by the illumination on the fence that only one was working.

With a little more buoyancy to his step, he went to the front door and knocked. He did not have to wait too long before being confronted by a rough looking woman, displaying all sorts of hand gestures, seeming to indicate that she was not enamoured with Coskin, for calling at such an hour.

From where I sat, I could see many more lights appearing at various windows, I assumed these were all siblings of O' Leary. I thought to myself rather callously, what if I just walked in and killed one of them, I wonder how he would feel.

It was about ten minutes before Coskin reappeared and again his departure was greeted by the same verbal abuse, as his entry. When he sat into the jeep, he said, 'The day I come back to arrest that man, I will have to bring reinforcements.'

He explained, 'O' Leary himself is a problem, but 'that battleaxe' that he is living with is as masculine as three men are. She told me,' he said, 'her husband never left the house all day and neither had the car. She refused to comment when I told her that what ever about him, the bonnet of the car was so hot that it was obvious that it had been driven recently.'

He was careful to point out that he needed to research the evidence a good deal more, before sending a file for prosecution. He correctly pointed out that, all he had so far was, my hearing a shout and old Frank seeing a car, coming from the scene.

The fact that the car here has also a defective light is little proof indeed. He knew of course that even a weak case could be enhanced by motive and clearly O' Leary had plenty.

The remainder of that evening was utilised in keeping a vigil, beside the body. We all took turns in staying awake, but in truth, I cannot remember much more of that night or the following day.

The only significant things that happened were the removal to the chapel by the undertaker, with whom I had negotiated, an extra fee to upgrade the coffin.

Then we had confirmation from Doctor Howard as to cause of death.

'Rosie died of a broken neck and not by drowning.' he declared.

Obviously, the whiplash nature of the careering wagon, had thrown her around so severely that she was dead before entering the stream.

The complications of the traveller's way of life sprung to the fore again the following day. Old Frank called and relayed the shock, findings of a church sub committee.

It decreed that Rosie was to be buried at the

far end of the graveyard, totally removed from the 'normal' people, Frank even went on refer to that particular plot, as the 'swamp'.

Apparently, only those without kin, or cast outs from society are buried there, also he suggested that proper records are not even kept after burial.

Both Willie and Kathleen seemed to accept this as 'par for the course', but I was in no way happy with this arrangement.

I quizzed Frank as to what my options were regarding the location. He said once Hawkins and the others had spoken, there was no room for discussion, even the priest cannot get involved. I asked Frank to tell me where Hawkins lived, and I would see if I could buy a plot in the main body of the churchyard direct from him.

I arrived at Hawkins home with the intention of having a civil conversation, but he anticipated my visit and the first words from his mouth put an end to any civility.

'You have some cheek, calling to my house, my home, to speak up for them tinkers.

Its bad enough, them looking for things themselves, besides a 'proper' person, speaking up for them, but then when all is said and done, you are not a proper person, sure aren't you just British scum, a 'blow in'. What more would I expect?

I will tell you', he said, as his tone turned to one of a condescending nature.

'A knacker will never be buried in our graveyard.'

Then without any further word, he just slammed the door in my face.

The ferocity of his tone and his warped, conviction of righteousness, sickened me to the stomach.

CHAPTER 35

The morning of the funeral, I went with Frank to see the plot that been allocated.

Frank and two other gravediggers set about digging. I was horrified and I broke down crying when I saw lumps of mud, old milk bottles and even bones from previous occupants filling the shovels. I then walked up to where Margo was buried, and I found myself talking quite loudly, hoping that she and her 'dancing Angel' would lift this cloud from me.

The church bell broke my train of thought, and I headed towards it's call. It is a wonder that the parishioners of Rahane even afforded the respect to allow the bells toll, for a person so low in their evaluation.

The church was reasonably full, with only an odd seat here and there. Willie and his family were at least given a front seat directly behind the nice, ornate, three quarter sized coffin.

I found a spare seat on the outside of a row about half way up the building. I initially kept my eyes towards the ground, mainly because I was not sure if I could fight away the tears, but also to avoid any accusative glances.

My entry did not go unnoticed, however,

as I had to pass the Viper. She was walking towards me giving out hymn sheets. As she approached me, she assumed a gleeful look that was evident to people in the next parish. In her eagerness to reach my side, she skipped at least three full rows, leaving them without any sheets.

In a loud whisper, she said, 'I knew it, I knew it, that child was doomed from the moment she met you, I hope you are happy now.'

I knew this was no place, to defend such an accusation, so I just took my seat and cringed.

Surely everybody who heard her knew that she was not right. I looked around and all I saw were heads bowed in indifference.

Father Turley started by thanking everybody for such a large attendance, he commiserated with the O' Donoghue family, for their loss and went on to explain, if explanation was needed as to the purpose of our attendance.

The ceremony then took the format of any ordinary, Sunday service. A few prayers here, a song there, nothing to make it stand out as a final farewell.

Father Turley, took his place in the pulpit, as if to deliver the eulogy, by saying; 'Normally, I would speak about the deceased with some historical knowledge, but in this case, I do not know much, it is enough to say that we give back to god a child, that I am sure, was loved by her family.

We will now continue with hymn, number thirty-four.'

'No, we will not.' I heard myself say. It was as if a Spirit had taken control of my being.

'I'm sorry.' Father Turley said.

I got up and walked towards the altar.

Nobody knew how to react as a noisy, uncomfortable atmosphere, descended on the entire chapel.

'You're sorry?!' I replied. 'That is the first emotional thing you have said or done, throughout this ceremony.'

By this time, I had reached the altar gates; I continued speaking as I opened them and within a second, I had arrived at the pulpit.

'You said, that you would normally, speak about a person, if you had some prior knowledge, the problem is you have plenty of prior knowledge, but you are too ashamed to speak of it.'

As if forced by a greater power, he just backed off, to allow me to address the auditorium.

'I will give you some prior knowledge', I shouted.

'We have here before us a young lady, called Rosie O' Donoghue. From her earliest days of childhood, she spent sixty days of each year of her young life in the company of you people of Rahane. She spent every school day of her life in the local school here in Rahane. She played, she grew and she cried... here in Rahane.

That should in ordinary circumstances, make her a member of the community of Rahane, but no, narrow mindedness, self-importance and fear make this community one of the sickest regimes, since the holocaust.

I feel very uncomfortable having to share a world with those who go from the cradle to the grave judging others, while at the same time never get to know themselves.

Rosie was a bright artistic, caring child who was put on this earth by the same Lord as everybody here in front of me. She had two legs, two arms, two eyes, she was physically, no different than you, or you, or you.

The fact that she was born into a traveller family should not make her an outcast. Her family may enjoy an alternative lifestyle, but they are still a family that, live, eat, sleep, breath and love as any other family here before me.

Today, they are a family in mourning, who have just lost a very important part of their lives. Their mourning is as real and their loss is as great as if Rosie belonged to any one of you.

Miss Francis, down there accused me of being responsible for the death of this young girl.

She said that Rosie O' Donoghue was doomed the moment she met me. ...Me?

I ask you all to look into your hearts, deep into your hearts and think.

If any good comes from such a tragic loss. It will be that other Rosie O' Donoghues of this world; will be given the respect they deserve, as a basic right.

Rosie O' Donoghue, was doomed all right, not the day she met me, but the day that she opened her eyes and saw Rahane.

Today, I ask the people of Rahane to open their eyes and see, Rosie O' Donoghue.

I looked down through my tears of emotion, and exhaustion to see, Sister O' Brien, the social worker, standing up and starting a slow appreciative, supporting applause.

To both my amazement and my delight, if delight was possible in this situation, I heard a similar reaction from Father Turley. He had by now returned to the front of the altar. Then as if by infection, other people, stood up and one by one, they too, all started clapping in unison, many had a tear in their eye some even cried inconsolably.

I could not see 'the Viper' any longer as she was hidden by the sea of bodies. I got immense satisfaction in knowing that this was, step one in the fight back.

I could see Hawkins, smirking as if he was to pour water on my flame. Immediately a thought came to me, I gestured to the crowd for silence and they responded instantly.

'It became known to me yesterday,' I continued. 'That this young girl is to be buried, at the swamp end of the graveyard, now this is a decision taken, by a select group of people who claim to represent you, the parishioners of Rahane. I ask you from this pulpit today, to take the first steps in; you're new found civil liberty, by offering her a place within the proper graveyard.' There was a unison of groans of approval, as I smiled at Kathleen.

'Wait.' Hawkins stood up.

'Forgive me father for speaking out in the church, but before Mister Roger's band wagon gets much more momentum, I would like to point out, to him, even if she were to be buried in a space in the main area, it is not possible. She can't have it you see, as all the spaces have been allocated.'

He shrugged his head with a matter of fact smile and said 'They're all taken, sorry.'

I leaned over the front of the pulpit and I gazed at him directly.

'Have I not got a grave, where my wife Margo, has been buried? Is it not in fact a double grave? Well can I not allocate that part of the double, to whom ever I chose?'

'Yes but not to a.....'

His impulsiveness turned to sheepishness, as he realised his isolation.

Father Turley, immediately spoke out. 'Well, then, that is settled before we now turn to Hymn thirty four, could I suggest to the grave diggers, to prepare the new resting place for our beloved sister. Now, I would like you all to stand and sing, *Abide with me*.'

In all the hassle and confrontations, I did not spend much time, with Kathleen and Willie, but it was probably for the best. As I am sure, our relative degrees of sorrow would have worked detrimentally, in any event.

The sight of Rosie, being lowered into the ground, brought a huge swell of sadness. All combination of questions ran through my mind, Why, Rosie?

What was the point of terminating her life after a mere, eleven years?

What sort of a God are you at all?

I took some semblance of comfort from the fact that she was to meet Margo, and I knew that, they would get on so well together.

After the ceremony, Sister O' Brien, came to my side and asked me how I was, I now know she was, enquiring of my emotional state, but I thought, at that time she knew something of my physical problem.

I answered, 'Won't be long until we are here again.'

Her shock triggered my realisation.

'Oh I am sorry, I misunderstood,' I blurted.

She linked my arm.

'Let me walk you to your car,' she requested.

When we reached the jeep, she immediately sat into the passenger seat.

'Now,' she inquired, 'what is exactly the prognosis?'

I felt quite free in telling her and in truth; I

needed someone to talk to. We spoke for over an hour and she really succeeded in making me 'think outside the box'.

As she left, she made me agree to call to see her shortly at the convent in Limerick.

'We have just spoken,' she said, 'of the material things that need sorting out, but there is a more important matter of the spiritual side.

God bless you, John.'

CHAPTER 36

The O' Donoghues remained on in the cottage, over the next few days, so I had to reuse the spare room.

Although unexplainable, Willie and indeed the two boys were never content under the solid roof. Willie kept sitting out on the front window ledge, and the boys just walked around aimlessly as if to escape the confinement.

Kathleen probably felt the same but for my benefit, she tried to integrate more. I knew however that this situation could not continue much longer.

Their confusion and lack of direction became unbearable, when I saw Willie burning the fragments of the broken wagon and Kathleen, salvaging the pots and pans that were strewn around the Sprid.

The day a truck with a crane removed the dead mare, I could stand it no longer.

I decided to implement the tasks that I had spoken to the Nun about. I duped Willie into believing, that I needed his advice in a transaction I was about to complete. I needed him to travel with me, in the jeep, and suggested that he brought Jimmy and Danny as well. I implied that it was to give Kathleen time to grieve alone.

My real reason was to visit an address that Coskin had given to me. It was an address of a Martin O' Sullivan, who lived about three miles outside the village. Martin was a car dealer, but was known at times to have a caravan or two in his stock.

As soon as we arrived, a well dressed, salesman met us. When I told him of my requirements, he promptly asked us to go around to the back of the showroom. Willie walked beside me not realising my ultimate intention, he must have assumed that I was looking for a caravan for myself.

The salesman showed me a caravan that was parked in the corner of the yard, it had a price tag on the window of three hundred pounds. He told me that, it had a good history.

'All it needs is a good cleaning; it will make a fine caravan for summer holidays.'

Straight away, Willie, spoke up. 'A good cleaning?' He shouted.

'A good cleaning, me hat, do you spect a man, like Mister Rogers here to be goin on his holidays, in dat wreck? Tis hardly fit for a dog. De underneath is full a rust and anyway tis far from summer time now wit Christmas not yet gone.

De true price a dat ting, is more like one hundred pounds.'

I was so embarrassed, not just for myself but also for the salesman, who had, afforded us the ultimate courtesy since our arrival.

I was no judge of anything mechanical, but if Willie did not like it then there was no point in continuing.

The salesman responded, 'Look what about if we split the price, say two hundred pounds?'

'One hundred and forty and not a penny more', was Willie's next offer.

The salesman said that before he could accept an offer that low, he would have to speak to his boss. He walked back into the showroom and left us alone.

'Willie, if the underneath is as rusty as you say, is there any point in buying it? I asked.

Willie said, 'don't be such *an amadan*, Mister Rogers. I figured dat man in his good clothes, was not going to kneel down and look underneath. De chassis is as clean as a whistle.'

The salesman returned, with a defeated smile.

'We have a deal.'

There was nothing more for me to do but pay the man. I then reversed the jeep around the building and Willie, hitched up the caravan.

'You got some bargain dere,' he declared. Possibly searching for a compliment about his bargaining skills.

Once again, I thought the 'negotiator' has come up trumps. Jimmy and Danny thought they had to travel in the caravan; such was their concept of travelling in a towed vehicle.

On the way back to the cottage I let Willie

drive the jeep, he was quite nervous at first, but then lessons learnt around the campsite of his youth started to pay off, and by the time we returned to the cottage he was doing quite well.

Kathleen met us at the door and quickly enquired about the caravan. I pretended to ignore her question and went into the caravan. I turned to both of them and I invited them in.

'Right', I said, 'here is the plan, in a few weeks, the growth in my side will defeat my resistance to live and I will be joining Rosie.'

Willie tried to interrupt, but Kathleen, subdued him.

I continued, 'I know there is no use in offering you the cottage, as I have seen the unrest, which you all find in a settled building. Also in this consideration is the fact that it will be a while before you will be an acceptable part of the Rahane community.

I am going to give you the jeep and of course this caravan. I will also arrange with a certain Nun, a Sister O' Brien, in Limerick to help you, if you find the running costs too expensive. I want you also to keep in touch with this Nun as she has also agreed to help Jimmy, Danny and eventually little Tommy, with their education.

Kathleen walked the short distance towards me and cried with joy as she hugged me.

I went on to say that, obviously it would be a few days before they would have the caravan ready for habitation, however in the meantime, they were welcome to stay in the cottage.

Kathleen once again thanked me and said that she would take up residence in the caravan as soon as possible.

'Den we will give you back your house key.'

The next few days, brought a significant deterioration in my health and I had to renew the prescription for the painkiller on two occasions.

The nights became longer as my sleeping became more difficult and I knew that time was indeed running out. The realisation that the end is approaching is indeed a frightening thought; it is a journey that one must make alone.

As I looked around the cottage, it was as if I was now a stranger there. No longer was there a warm appeal, the welcome aura or the fond memories.

'That's it.' I thought to myself, 'Must get my affairs in order, not long left now.

I will dispose of it. Whatever I do with it now is fruitful.

Cannot take it with me. I cannot give it to the O' Donoghues, life would be hell for them living among the bitterness, the hatred and the memories.'

Then suddenly, a strange smile came over my face, a devious little plan was hatching in my head, here is a chance to, 'Let the cat among the pigeons.'

The thought of my impending conspiracy, gave me an extra spring in my step, and with my newfound adrenalin rush, I got into the Jeep, and with Willie O' Donoghue as a driver, I headed for an auctioneers office in Killaloe.

I briefed Willie on his part and we went over the script five or six times.

'Geez, I hope I can do dis', he said as he laughed at the idea.

I waited eagerly for the 'Rahane Gazette' to hit the streets; I even ventured into Foley's to pick up a copy, just to test the reactions of the locals. I did not have to wait long for confirmation of interest. Foley and Hawkins were together at the door, Foley became the mouthpiece for the pair as Hawkins, was not man enough to talk.

'Tis a pity you went to the trouble of getting an out of town auctioneer to handle the sale of the ould home place.' He declared.

'Sure there are many people within the village here would have given you a fair price with out the need for a public auction.'

'Oh I am so sorry, I never thought of that, but what is done is done.' I said.

'We will see what happens on Wednesday. You might still own it.'

I indicated as I walked away, he followed me and attempted a more subtle approach.

'Look.' He went on to say.

'We heard about your illness, and a sale by auction is a stressful business, you could still withdraw it and sell it to one of us privately.

We are only thinking of your welfare, you know.'

I looked into his eyes and suddenly, thirty pieces of silver flashed through my mind.

'There is one thing,' I asked, 'If you want to make things a little more comfortable, rather than risk the Irish weather and hold the auction outdoors, would it be possible to hold it in the courthouse, It would be easier to hear the auctioneer and the ...bidders.'

He looked at Hawkins, who gave the briefest nod of approval.

'Consider that done, nothing much happens on a week night anyway, I will make sure the room is ready and the seats laid out,' he replied.

CHAPTER 37

Wednesday, finally arrived, and I did not think that there were so many residents in Rahane. All the locals, including Father Turley and even Mick Coskin attended. Every seat was taken, every inch of floor space was occupied, I chuckled when I heard 'Dan the Man' saying, 'Begorrah if any more people come in, they will have to tear the paper from the walls to make room.'

I noted also that in keeping with my expectation, the entire community council, were dutifully seated across the front row.

The auctioneer called the proceedings to order.

'Well,' he said, 'I have never seen such a crowd turn up for the sale of any property in my life, and I hope you all have your cheque books to hand.

The property we are about to sell is a lovely little cottage on the edge of Rahane, encompassing the west side of the Shannon down to the Sprid. It is a lovely property self-contained on an acre of land, listed on the land registry as property 297 in the county of Clare. The property is for sale with one month's notice of vacant possession and currently owned freehold by Mister Jonathan Rogers, who is here seated beside me. It goes on the market with a guide price of seventeen thousand pounds. Right then, bid me, and start me where you like.'

I looked at the crowd and thought, 'This is it, let the fun begin.'

Hawkins raised his hand and announced, 'Twelve thousand.'

A voice from the middle shouted, 'thirteen.'

Somewhere else came a cry 'fourteen', until it reached twenty thousand.

I heard Dan the Man; mention that offer is from Ould Jer Lainey, 'Sure haven't he a grand daughter that is getting married next month, it would be an ideal, home for her particularly as she is already in the family way.'

Hawkins and the rest of the council must have thought the same as they were resigned to not contesting the bid.

Now I thought here we go, I put my hand to my left ear as, as a signal and waited for the plan to 'kick in'.

'Twenty two,' a voice from the back door shouted.

I swear that the actual room moved because of the instant almost choreographed head movement of the entire audience.

The answer to the puzzle as to the identity of the bidder was quickly, distributed to the front row, it was of course, Willie.

Miss Francis immediately stood up and announced that that bid cannot be accepted.

'You can't sell to a traveller, where will he get the money?'

Quite correctly, the auctioneer interjected, 'I must ask you to sit down madam It is a criminal offence to bid at a public auction without having the funds in place to 'back up' the bid, the man appears over the age of eighteen and if that is the final bid then I will sell the property to the 'twenty two bidder.'

Hawkins, went into a secretive huddle with his fellow councillors and raised his hand, 'Twenty three,' Again, I put my hand to my ear and Willie shouted, 'Twenty five, Sir.'

Hawkins looked across his line for approval 'Twenty six,' he said as he gave a daggered look at O' Donoghue.

Once more, a hand movement caused an instant response, 'tirty, tree!'

'Thirty three, I have and I am selling to that big man at the door.

Do I have another bid from the front?' The auctioneer requested.

I knew that on no account could the locals afford to allow a member of the travelling community a foot hold in their sacred little 'cocoon'. They had to keep going, some raised voices were heard from the front, panic was setting in... It was apparent that they were trying to calculate how much each other, could afford.

Hawkins eventually stood up and blurted out, 'thirty four.'

This time my hands remained where they were, and the auctioneer closed the bidding.

'Sold to the gentleman in the front row, for thirty four thousand pounds, could you come forward with your deposit sir?

All that is left for me to say, is thank you all for your attendance and that concludes the sale.'

As the people funnelled out, I knew they were shocked at the price the cottage had achieved. I could hear many saying that; it was over twice its value.

Eventually when the hall cleared, all that remained was the entire community council, arguing over the ridiculous price they had just paid for the property. Each dumbfounded at the events of the past half hour.

Coskin, the auctioneer and I were standing at the opposite side of the table, like two teams preparing for a rugby scrum. Willie quickly joined us to even up the line.

'My Willie you are a dark horse,' I deliberately uttered, quite loudly.

'I would not have placed you as a man of money?'

'Sure Mister Rogers, I had to shtop when the price went above tirty tree, cause before I came here,' he pretended to count on his fingers.

'That me self and de Misses tageter,

worked out that even tho, we would love ta own de cottage, all we have in our savins is tirty tree pounds and four shillings.'

Hawkins eyes lit up like a blowtorch, and said, 'thirty three pounds....thirty three pounds....You fool it was thirty three **thousand** pounds.'

Willie just looked in a matter of fact fashion, as if suddenly realising his error and said.

'Well wasn't it a fine thing that I didn't't get it then....But then I could always have paid by ...A travellers cheque...' With a coy laugh he shrugged his shoulders and walked away. Coskin turned his back on the now squabbling mob and looked directly at me, as he said, 'You set this up, you scoundrel, and remind me to never play poker with you.'

'Come on,' I said, 'Time for a drink.

CHAPTER 38

By now word had gone around the village, of the duping of the council and I knew it was only a matter of time when, their reign, would eventually become untenable.

Mike Foley, on the other hand seemed to congratulate me on the price, more than on the mode of obtaining it. I started to realise that many of the people in Rahane, were stuck in a rut of submission, where only the 'elite' few seemed to make the decisions.

If someone could break their grip, then Rahane might in fact be a nice little village to live in.

Maybe, I thought, have I initiated the seeds of freedom?

Foley gave Coskin and I the first round on the house and we headed to Coskin's favourite spot in the 'Nook', just behind the piano. It was quite a vantage point as he could see and yet not be seen. After a few minutes, he revealed to me that he had received word back from the procedures office and said that they felt the evidence, was too weak to arrest Josie O' Leary, or go to trial.

'Unless, he either admits the incident or indeed an eyewitness comes forward, then he has only his God to answer to.'

This maddened me a little, but I knew whatever the result, it would not bring back Rosie.

Never has the phrase, 'speak of the devil' been so apt, as Coskin's eyes directed me to look towards the door. The sight of O'Leary walking in suddenly awoke the anger within me as I contemplated some very evil deeds.

'What right have you,' I thought, 'to walk this earth when Rosie, can not?'

Had he collapsed and died at that moment, I would have danced with joy.

As the night progressed, I drank quite a large amount of alcohol in an attempt to numb the hatred and contempt; I had built up inside me. Then to further intensify my hatred, I had an encounter that could have really pushed me over the edge.

On a visit to the men's room, Peadar Scanlon, the drinking friend of Josie O' Leary, approached me. I wanted to ignore him, as I felt any meeting would be confrontational. However, I know now that our meeting was not coincidental. He put his arm on my shoulder as I was about to return to the bar and he said.

'Mister Rogers, I need to talk to you. I want to clear my conscience. Despite what you think, I am not a bad man and now I know for certain that neither are you.

If this goes to court I will deny, what I am

about to say.

The whole world knows that we were at the campsite the time Josie, had his 'goolies' burned off, I swear to you now that we had decided to go there only to frighten the travellers and hope they would take the hint and leave.

Josie, however saw the little girl and fancied his chances of raping her in front of her parents. We were as disgusted, and shocked, as anyone, after all I have a ten year old and a six-year-old daughter and I would kill anyone who would touch them. We definitely made a pact not to hurt anyone. We were about to intervene, but then the young girl, defended herself. I was so glad and I still feel that Josie got what he deserved.

However, the other night when we, were drinking in here, Josie, took my car from outside and went up to the cottage with a rag and a bottle of kerosene. It was his intention to set fire to your house, it turned out that it rained so heavily, that the rag would not light. In his infuriation, he untied the horse and made it bolt down the lane.

He said, twas a pity he didn't know the child was in the wagon at the time cause he said, her death was far too easy.

I insisted that he should tell Coskin of this, but he replied, 'No one saw him doing it, so he will deny it.'

Scanlon went on to mention that it was his

car that was used and O' Leary was not above pointing fingers, if he was cornered.

At this point, I could see genuine fear in his eyes, 'I must go now,' he continued, 'If O' Leary even knew I was talking to you, I tell you,' he said emphatically, 'That man would stop at nothing....'

I rejoined Coskin, but I do not remember any of the conversation that ensued. I know however that I attempted to drink away my anger, as the night slowly became a blur.

CHAPTER 38

I woke up the following morning in the cottage, nursing a massive headache. I knew by drinking my 'magic lotion' that it would not cease. I was fully aware of the difference between, physical pain and a hangover. I was still dressed as I had been for the funeral. I noticed the shoes that I was wearing covered in mud.

'My,' I thought, 'I must have walked home last night.' I looked at the clock and realised that it was nearer noon than morning. I struggled to the bathroom, feeling so feeble and ill that the thought crossed my mind that, maybe this was to be my final day. I struggled to disrobe and found my pants to be very obstinate. I fell over on two occasions and on one of them, I hit my elbow so hard against the table, as I sat there clutching it, I thought I was about to die. When I eventually got to my feet, I was quite relieved to once again reach the couch and find some respite from the pain.

My eyes drifted in and out of different stages of blurriness as I attempted to look again at the clock.

Then suddenly, they clicked into perfect focus as I realised all was not right in the room.

I looked at the mantelpiece and spotted two horseshoe nails that formerly supported the old gun. I searched around the room, to see if I could find it.

I then got up and passed the pain barrier like a sprinter at the tape.

I went to the cabinet where the bullets were stored to find that at least five bullets were missing. I sat down at the table put my head in my hands and tried to take in what was happening.

I did not have to wait long to get some answers.

A knock at the door and a faint, call announced Coskin's arrival.

As he stood there his jovial, demeanour was missing.

He said, 'Now we've got problems,' then he paused to allow the words to sink in.

'Mick', I replied, 'I don't remember a thing, how bad is it?'

'It's pretty bad John, pretty bad indeed.' He paused for a moment, and shook his head.

'We didn't find the gun,' he looked over the fireplace and asked, 'Have you any idea where it is?'

I still did not remember a thing, but I knew enough, not to offer inebriation as an excuse.

'What happens next?' I asked.

'Well this time it's out of my control or jurisdiction. Murder is dealt with by the Limerick detectives and the Limerick court.'

'Murder?' I stammered. He ignored my surprise and continued, 'you changed the outlook of many people in the last few days, John; now they will just go back to where they were, full of their original, bigotry and hatred.'

I had no option but to ask him to give me his account of the happenings, as I genuinely had no recollection of what had happened. I assumed of course that somehow I had taken the gun and shot, someone, possibly Josie O' Leary.

'It was Josie O' Leary?' I enquired.

'Yes', he said. 'Shot at least five times, two in the head, one in the heart and two in the groin.

All at close range and with a 303, have you any idea where your gun is?'

'Did anyone see, exactly what happened?' I asked still trying to bring back some memory.

'Yes, Josie O' Leary's wife saw it all, she said about midnight she heard the dogs barking, she looked out and saw Josie, stumbling up the path towards the house, just as he got within view, she said she saw a man jump out from one of the old scrapped cars in the driveway, the man too looked drunk, there was a brief exchange of words and the assailant just lifted the gun, pointed it straight at him and shot him, as he fell to the ground the man continued shooting him.

When she shouted out to him, he just looked at her and walked slowly away carrying the weapon by his side.

She said she got a clear look at him and that is why we are here now.

'The only thing we need to tie the case up, is the gun, have you any idea where it is?

Have you the keys of the jeep? Maybe it is in there.

Before I could answer, Kathleen, burst through the doorway, 'Mister Rogers, what are we going to do?'

'Don't worry,' I said.

At this stage, it dawned on me that I was standing in front of her wearing only my underwear.

'Let me get some clothes on and Mick here will advise me what to do.'

'I think it is best you return to the caravan, Misses O' Donoghue, I will call to see you in a few moments.' Coskin instructed.

I went to the bathroom, still wondering how I managed to get to O' Leary's house and back, given the intoxicated state I was in, was I capable of murdering someone as callously as Coskin described.

Had my sense of feeling above the law, being too flippant? What happens next?

Do I face the ridicule of being chastised in court? Do I spend my days in prison? Oh what a roller coaster.

When I re-entered the room, a strange man in a suit was now by Coskin's side.

'This is Detective O' Callaghan from

Limerick; he will be overseeing the case.'

A brief nod in either direction confirmed the introduction.

'Is that your Jeep, Sir? He asked. Without waiting for an answer, he continued, 'Can you furnish the keys of the same vehicle?'

How officious I thought, dealing with him is going to be a barrel of laughs. I searched the drawer where the keys normally were and they were missing.

I noticed Coskin, going outside as I tried to remember where I had them last and my memory, stopped at the graveside.

I do not remember driving home, so conversely I cannot remember where I had put the keys. Almost immediately, the riddle was answered as Coskin came through the doorway, waving them aloft.

'They were left in the ignition', he said, 'but there's no sign of the weapon.'

'Where is the gun?' The detective demanded.

'Do you', he continued, 'Realise the trouble you could be in, if you don't tell me where it is?'

Surely, I thought, that the scale of trouble I am already in is not going to increase dramatically, by the non-production of the gun.

'I really, don't know', I said, 'I must have dumped it somewhere.'

'Dumped it somewhere?' Was the bemused question, they both asked together.

'Do you have something to do with the incident as well?' The detective asked.

He then broke systematically into the ritual, caution, whereby anything I say, may be used in evidence, etc.

At this stage, I was more confused than ever, so I asked.

'Am I going to be arrested, straight away?'

They both looked at each other totally bemused. Then Coskin, spoke up. 'John, is there something you are hiding from us?'

He continued, 'It would do Willie O' Donoghue, no good if you are trying to shield him.

'Willie?!' I shouted. 'What has he got to do with it?'

'I told you already,' Coskin replied, 'Misses O' Leary clearly identified Willie as the perpetrator.'

I was naturally relieved, that I had not done this, but then my thoughts turned to Willie.

'Where is he now?' I asked.

'I told you that also', Coskin replied, 'he has been taken to Limerick, to be officially charged.'

'...Because of who he is', O' Callaghan replied, 'it is very unlikely if he will make bail.'

I immediately corrected him, in a strong accusative manner. 'You mean, not who he is, but what he is.'

Without any reaction, he just reiterated, their need to find the gun and then made his exit.

Coskin followed him, but before doing, said 'John, for heaven's sake get some sleep, you look dreadful.'

With those complimentary words of wisdom, I struggled, to the couch and in minutes, I was fast asleep.

My mind did not follow my body into the restful state however, as I could see Willie, in a cell, Kathleen, alone and lost, pacing up and down the caravan, knowing that the responsibility of a young family, now lay squarely on her shoulders.

Was there much more distress life could throw at these people? Then there was the thought, of the entire village laughing at me for being such a fool. For a brief moment, Josie O' Leary did enter my mind but not I will admit in any grief-stricken fashion.

I did not wake up until the following morning and in truth, surprised my self as to the duration of my sleep.

A new day, I thought and possibly a new set of problems. To my surprise, the fire had an enthusiastic, glowing flame. It was obvious that it had only been lit within the past hour or so. The architect of this thoughtfulness was no doubt either Frank or Kathleen. Then, I lifted myself up on to one arm and immediately spotted a selection of my clothes, including underwear, neatly folded on a stool near the sink, my shoes were spotlessly polished and a selection of preparatory dishes, were laid neatly on the table. It seemed a bit surreal, as if I was the heroine in beauty and the beast, although one look in the bathroom mirror and I would have been more correctly cast as the former.

The layout of the table seemed well thought out, but I was not sure if I had any food in stock to make use of the design. I need not have worried however because, when I returned from the bathroom, a breakfast and a hot mug of coffee, was now augmenting the display.

I looked in the main bedroom, the spare room, and then outside the front door for confirmation as to the identity of my host. There was no one to be found anywhere.

After breakfast, I washed the dishes, and then I spent the next hour attending to my self-beautification.

I was now devoid of any formal idea as to what I should do for the rest of the day. My rational had deserted me. It possibly did not matter in any event because any plans I had made lately were of no use, as some crisis seemed to arise that made them redundant.

Old Frank called at some point that morning. He had only just heard of the incident from the previous night and he too expressed a cautious, satisfaction as to the demise of O' Leary. He also mentioned that Willie was formerly charged late last evening and was refused bail.

'He is to be remanded in court until next Tuesday. Coskin asked me to tell you that Willie, is 'holding up' well, but that he is strangely numb about the entire episode. Coskin described him as a broken man resigned to whatever fate was to befall him.'

I decided there and then to go and visit him, that is if visiting was allowed.

I thought it better not to tell Kathleen of my pending visit, but I had to pause for a moment as I passed the caravan, to thank her for the breakfast etc.

She looked strangely, bemused as she nodded acceptance. I felt guilty, not telling her where I was going, or even not taking the time to console her further.

'No matter how strong any person is,' I thought, 'No one could handle, with any degree of sanity, the loss of a daughter coupled with the immediate, separation from a spouse. I wondered also, as to what her take on Willie's actions were.

How near to prophetic, were her words as I think back to her initial description of her husband, when I met Kathleen for the very first time.

'He'd die forty times rader dan let antin happen to any of de childer.'

CHAPTER 40

On the journey to Limerick, I wondered would I have to somehow exchange the caravan for a horse drawn wagon once again as it was unlikely that Kathleen could drive a mechanical vehicle.

I thought about the gun. I should have forseen the risk Willie posed. Kathleen had already warned me of his paternal volatility and the potential revenge he could extract. I should have taken back the cottage spare key, when they returned to live in the caravan.

'Hindsight is a great thing.'

Then of course, there was the opinions of the villagers. To them, it must look like every argument I had, put forward to counteract the negativity, of the traveller life style, was now seriously flawed.

When I got to the gaol in Limerick, its sheer size overawed me. To a degree, I was glad that it was of such magnitude as to allow Willie, some sense of space to ease his claustrophobia.

On entry, I noticed that visiting time was strictly enforced and only available between the hours of three and four in the afternoon. It being still morning, I utilised the time to call to the dispensary at the hospital, to replenish my painkiller.

It was such a distressful feeling, returning to the spot where only days before I had held Rosie, in my arms. Her girlish giggle that took away my own sense of grief still reverberates in the back of my mind.

As I entered through the gates of the hospital, I saw Sister O' Brien walking out from the sector; marked intensive care. I was just about to beep the horn to attract her attention when I saw a young couple following her on to the car park. I had never seen the woman before but I immediately recognised the male as Peadar Scanlon. They were huddled in deep conversation so I desisted from any further contact and simply went to the relevant unit to collect my elixir.

I returned to the gaol, in time to fall into a queue of mothers with screaming kids, poorly dressed men chewing 'backy', and a few over dressed men and women, with brief cases. After a brief security check, we were all ushered into a room, the size of a football pitch. There were rows of tables lined from one end to the other.

The white-collar brigade made their way towards another room, but the rest of us had to take designated places at these long tables. We were then asked by various prison officers, as to which 'convict' we were here to see. Armed with the relevant information, they then in turn returned with the requested inmate.

I saw Willie being led through the lower

door, and a cold unforgiving finger pointed him towards me. He sat at the opposite side of the table, as were his instructions.

'How's Kathleen and the childer?' He asked immediately.

I reassured him that they were as well as could be and obviously missing him.

I deliberately avoided the topic of the killing as I was not sure of his mental state and it was conceivable to expect his apparent calmness turning volatile.

However, I felt comfortable in asking him the whereabouts of the gun. Before answering, he looked around so suspiciously, I was surprised that one of the overseeing prisoner officers did not approach us to enquire about the deviousness of our conversation.

He then spoke in the softest whisper he could muster. At one part, I was condemned to some lip reading to complete the sentences.

'Well ya know, de old shed behind da house where de old woman used to milk de cow, in dere is an old long stool wit broken legs, tis under dat, I didn't have much time ta plank it so ya mite, dump it in the river when deres no one about.'

I was a little surprised by his suggesting that I get involved.

In the broader scheme of things, did it really matter if the gun was located or not.

He continued to tell me that the state had supplied a barrister to defend him in court.

However, he did not at any stage realise or even fear pending conviction.

At one stage, he did refer to the fact that Josie O' Leary was not arrested for both the attack on Rosie and her subsequent murder.

'If he gets away wit dose tings den I'll definitely get away wit dis.'

'My god,' I thought, 'does he not understand that in this case, there is an eyewitness, or what false hope has his barrister given him?

As the bell signalled time up on the visitation, he asked me to pass on his love to Kathleen and the boys. He also mentioned that he would prefer if they did not come to see him in this environment.

'De court case is only two days away,' he said, 'Shur, I'll be home straight after dat.'

As I left the gaol that day, I wondered was he heading for a huge shock.. I could not condone what he had done, but I truly believed he felt he was acting justifiably.

I know that in my drunken state, I too could have killed O' Leary, but I am certain that with a clear head, I would not however.

For the last mile of the journey, back to the cottage, I thought about the gun and I became paranoid, about cars travelling behind me, or any movement around me. I deduced that the detectives would be clever enough to assume that Willie would tell me about the location of the weapon and place me under surveillance.

It was the time of day between, light and dark when I got to the cottage, but I decided to wait some time before searching the 'out house'.

Frank called in briefly, but I am sure I made him feel uncomfortable, by not entering into any deep conversations with him, as I would normally do. The anxiousness to verify the location of the weapon preceded all other thoughts.

It did cross my mind at one stage to tell Frank about the gun, but I felt I could always, tell him later if I needed to.

When he finally left, I waited a mere minute, to initiate the search. I checked all around with a fearful eye, as I walked towards the rear of the cottage.

There was a part of me that wished that the damn thing was not there. I lifted the old stool and exactly as he had described, it lay there ready to do more damage, if it were called upon.

I scurried back indoors, dangling the thing as if it had a mind of its own and if let loose would wreak further havoc on society.

I was still not sure as to what exactly I was going to do with it, but Willie's suggestion to dump it in the river seemed a logical option.

I examined it with a morbid stare, almost expecting to see some particles of Josie O' Leary's blood or hair on the barrel.

I took off the magazine, and emptied it, on

to the table; it was still full of unspent bullets, as if ready for another onslaught. I thought this was rather strange and I wondered why he would have the presence of mind after committing a brutal murder, to reload the thing.

I went to the cabinet to count the remaining bullets, and to my total confusion, there were only five bullets missing from the box, so with the reintroduction of the contents of the magazine, the box was now once again full.

I checked as much as I could as to the similarity of the new with the old and as far as I could be certain, they were a perfect match. Therefore, my conundrum was where Willie did, get the bullets that he used to shoot, the victim? On the other hand, did he in fact, shoot him at all?

Then what about the eye witness? And why did he hide the gun?

I had to assume for the sake of carrying out any further investigation, that Misses O' Leary was mistaken as to the identity of the gunman.

What do I do now? I cannot tell Coskin, because then the blame will revert to me, but then I cannot be guilty either as this gun does not appear to be the murder weapon.

I had to meet him however, to positively, establish how I managed to get home, the night of the shooting, I needed even if for sanity purposes, to account for those missing moments. It was appearing as if the more answers, I came up with, proportionately the more questions were being revealed.

I went into the bedroom to get my coat to travel to find Coskin. The court case was the day after tomorrow and I needed to find out what really happened, both to me and to O' Leary, as soon as possible.

As I put one arm in the sleeve of the coat, I turned sharply in the room and I immediately went all-light headed, and fell to the floor.

'Oh no.' I pleaded, 'please God, if you exist, don't take me just now, I have some unfinished business to complete. I do not remember, getting on to the bed and I certainly do not remember any further happenings for that entire night.'

I woke up the following morning with another empty bottle of pain reliever on the floor. I knew that my body, was displaying the tell tale signs of imminent shutdown.

I wasted no further time in calling to the Police station where I met Coskin.

As soon as he saw me, he immediately rushed to the door and assisted me to a chair by the desk.

This to me was the confirmation that the external paintwork was depicting the true shape of the inside of the building.

When I started to tell him that I was concerned about Willie, he stared at me as if in disbelief.

'Jonathan Rogers,' he demanded.

'You are a very sick man, why not stop worrying about others and think about yourself? You need to get some rest, if you wish I will drive you back home.'

I rejected his offer and did not want to waste any time in small talk.

I told him all that I had discovered the previous night.

At first he did not seem to want to talk of Willie's predicament, he felt that it was in the hands of the detectives, but the bullets and the gun did intrigue him somewhat.

'I will tell you what I'll do.' He said. 'You go back home and shortly I will call to the cottage and I will, take the gun and the box of shells, to Limerick and mention your findings.'

'You then get a good night's sleep because you may be asked to give evidence about this find, at the court tomorrow. Right now, I am doubtful if you are physically capable of the stress involved.'

'Don't you worry about me.' I replied, 'To a degree, I have been the catalyst for a lot of this misfortune and I have little time to put it right.

The only thing I ask Mick is can I travel with you tomorrow, as I don't feel up to driving.'

'Of course John, I was going to suggest that myself anyhow.' He replied.

On the way back to the cottage, I called to the caravan. The first thing, I noticed was the transformation from the damp, unused smell to a clean, habitable environment. The little gas fire was barely lighting, but the glow was perfectly adequate to placate any element of coldness.

Kathleen deduced immediately from my look of approval, that I was impressed by her homemaker skills.

'Tis indeed a big step up, since the auld wagon. Sure de boys don't know demselves, as we have so much space 'tis unreal. Rosie would have loved it.' 'Yes I am sure she would,' I said, 'she did have a likeness for the grander things in life.'

'Speakin of Rosie,' she interrupted, 'when she was at your place before the undertaker came, I took back the flower dat you placed in her hands, dis flower was something she had since she was four years old, she got it from my mother, as a gift to show her dat beauty fades away, but love lives forever.'

She handed me the flower as she continued, 'She chose you Sir, and believe me she knew you were a good person, you were de only person, aside from her family, dat she ever loved.'

She then placed her hands on mine and said, 'She knew all along, what was goin to happen, she knew dat de two of you could not be tageter in dis world, so she died to be wit you, in a place where no one will be judging or no one will be judged.'

The next statement was the most comforting I have ever heard, 'She is waitin for ya, Mister Rogers, waitin for ya.'

CHAPTER 41

I was back in the cottage, kneeling down trying to light the fire, when I realised that I had not once mentioned Willie, during my visit to Kathleen. Then again, she did not make any mention of it either. I assumed that the barrister had made some contact with her and reassured her of Willie's state of mind, but if that were the case… It made me wonder as to the calibre of this legal eagle.

'He was,' I deduced, 'either, brilliant or a fool.'

After lighting the fire, I needed to clutch onto the wall, in my effort to stand up, as the pangs of pain became ever more regular. My body colour was changing more frequently than the Irish weather. My entire body heat was fluctuating and my chest was contracting to excruciating pain. I sat on the couch and clutched the little plastic rose, in a meagre effort of comfort.

I took a pen and paper and wrote a goodbye note to old Frank,

My dear Frank, you have always been a good friend not just to Maggie and me, but also to her family, for a long time before that.

After the money has been deposited from the Sale of the cottage, I want you to call to a Sister O' Brien at the Daughters of Charity, in Limerick. I have arranged for her to give you some money to help you make your life more comfortable. I also have put a few bob aside for old Mo.

You might try to examine the possibility that if you look up the grave register, at the church, you might be able to find someone willing to sell a plot, near to Maggie and Rosie.

Sister O' Brien, has the rest of my instructions, Thanks … Your friend, Jonathan.

P.S. Make sure this plastic rose is with me at the end.

CHAPTER 42

The following morning, I hardly remember the trip to Limerick; it was so uncomfortable, not because of Coskin's driving, but the many pains that now afflicted me.

He said, 'I brought the gun to Limerick and the detectives mentioned that it was a vital piece of information.'

He added. 'They would make the defence council aware of it.

You never know what the jury will make of it, but if it were not for the eye witness, the prosecution case would be very shaky.'

The court case got underway on schedule, and the jury had already been selected before the *audience* were allowed in.

Willie stood motionless, beside two well-dressed men, one holding a file of papers. This man looked quite elderly, but it was difficult to see clearly from my vantage point in the gallery.

At a guess, I would have put him in his very late sixties. There was also a strange look of familiarity about him. The other was not much more than a teen.

I looked around and saw many regular faces from Rahane, but some whose names eluded me.

I did recognise Hawkins, Foley and Scanlon. All no doubt hoping the case would go against Willie.

A Garda superintendent, read the charges and he then addressed the jury; 'This is a relatively simple case,' he pleaded. 'On one hand, we have a caring family man, a father of seven children and a husband to a caring wife. A man that never had any run in with the law in his life. A man that went to his local bar for a drink before returning home and on that fore mentioned trip home was brutally attacked and shot, not just once but five times and in plain view of his adoring wife.'

'On the other hand we have, a man, of no fixed abode, a traveller, who was recently arrested for beating up some young children in broad daylight. A man with a violent history. A man who took the law into his own hands, by stealing a gun - this gun', as he raised my gun from a table.

'A gun that, he procured by breaking into a neighbours house and stole. He then picked out with maximum calculation, his victim, after blaming him for some incident or other and shot him dead, in a cold-blooded act of revenge.

We have the motive, the weapon, and the witness and now I introduce to you...The perpetrator.' He pointed directly at Willie.

Almost everything he said was

incomprehensible to Willie, who was still looking around as if he was sitting on the sand at a seaside.

His barrister had to shock him into reality, as he appeared puzzled at something.

'Your honour,' he said, 'We were never told of the locating of any weapon.

In order to correctly defend my client I have to be versed with all the evidence. This blatant attempt to side-swipe the jury is grounds to apply for a miss trial,' he threatened.

'I have to agree with you,' the judge commented.

'I would like the jury to disregard the evidence of the gun, for the moment anyway.'

He then directed his attention to the prosecution bench and said, 'Inspector, there are certain undertones to this case that I am not very happy with and I suggest you and your team realise the density of the thin ice you are skating on. As a result I am recessing the court for one hour to allow council to gain access to all the relevant background and to further consult with his client.'

He brought down the gavel with a ferocity that had intolerance written all over it.

Willie and the barrister disappeared through a door, just behind the judge. My eyes drifted back to the swelling ranks of detectives that were gathering around the prosecution table and one sensed the scent of blood as they further conspired to make sure this 'traveller' became the fall guy for this crime.

It is indeed a travesty that power, when in the wrong hands, seems to flourish, Margo used to say, 'Give an angel a horse and he will ride to hell.'

As for my take on the situation, all sorts of questions were forming in my head; did they not understand what I had said about the gun?

The sheer arrogance and ignorance to decree that Willie was a poor parent, so poor in fact to be inferior to Josie O' Leary? Are we facing another battle of bigotry? When will it ever end?

At this juncture, Coskin had by now joined his peers, but he seemed to be arguing bitterly with the detectives. It was a very brief altercation as I then noticed the inspector handling the affair, pointing a finger consigning him to the exit door.

Obviously, a rank pulling exercise, but I was glad to see at least that some men, like Coskin still try to operate with integrity.

I immediately left my seat and met him at the foot of the stairway.

'John,' Coskin said, 'I've let you down, I've let myself down and more disastrously, I've let Willie down.

These guys here are just looking for an easy quick conviction and by so doing are getting one more traveller off the streets, and I have supplied the rod to beat our own backs. I must see the defence council, because I now know that your findings were never relayed to him.'

It still bothered me as to why Willie was not being more defensive. Whatever gun he used was clearly not my one, unless he had access to more bullets.

I was still swayed to thinking that he was innocent. 'Then if he did not commit the deed, why did he hide the gun?'

'Come on Coskin,' I urged. 'You are the legal brain here. Can you throw any light on all of this?

'To be truthful', I continued, 'I am just as likely to be in the frame for committing this murder as Willie, it is my gun they hold as the exhibit, I have no recollection of my actions and more worryingly I am not sure of Misses O' Leary, and her evidence.

'Did she in fact get a clear look at the gunman?'

I continued, 'The one definite inconsistency in her statement was, that after the auction, I know Willie and Kathleen, went back to the caravan together and while under her control, Willie would not drink to excess.

You said that Misses O' Leary mentioned that the gunman seemed, very drunk.'

'So what are you saying?' He enquired.

'I am saying that, I tick more boxes, than Willie; motive, being drunk, memory loss and owning the gun.' I continued.

'I have been meaning to ask you. Can you fill in the latter end of the night of the auction, the night of the killing? I got so drunk; I do not remember a thing.'

'Well, he said I am not much help, because around ten o' clock, most people had left the bar, it being a week night and all. The only people still there were the two of us, the Bodran Milward, Dan the man and Peadar Scanlon, Even Josie O' Leary had gone home.'

'Ten O' clock,' I enquired, 'But the shooting didn't happen until after midnight.'

'You are right.' he said, 'He must have gone somewhere else, before he went home, in any event, Rachel Foley tried to call a taxi for you, but the only one working that night, was Johnnie O' Gorman, but he was not available, as he had to run young, Mary Scanlon, Peadar's, six year old daughter to Limerick hospital.

Apparently, she fell down two flights of stairs. When the news came through, Peadar, left to try and arrange a spin to Limerick to join his wife.'

'Yes,' I said, 'I knew she was there I saw them yesterday, coming out of intensive care.'

'Then what happened to me?' I quickly implored.

'You fell asleep here for a short time; you were going to wait for Johnnie O' to come back from Limerick. But to be truthful, I think as soon as I left you drove yourself home, how you managed it I am not sure.'

'Mick, I wonder if there is any way I can

talk to Willie? I need to ask him some questions; I need to ask him out straight, I need to know what he knows and why he is so relaxed and secretive about everything.

I hope that his belief in me may sway him to tell me for sure what happened.'

Coskin, went into some rooms, at the side of the courtroom and reappeared almost immediately, and signalled to me to return with him.

The barrister and a uniformed Guard, were sitting in the room, Willie was standing up, looking out through a barred up window.

Coskin said, 'I have cleared it to allow Mister Rogers, here to speak with the accused.

Neither of the men, made any objection, but I knew Coskin had not enough time to seek any type of clearance. He pretended to be abrupt, as he said to me, 'The guard and I will be outside the door, you have three minutes.'

'As soon as they had left, the barrister got up to face me, he said, 'Mister Rogers, we meet again.'

I looked at him for a moment and then, 'the penny dropped'.

I recognised him as Mister Hay, the solicitor that failed to turn up, when Willie was accused of beating up the school kids.

'I owe you an apology', he immediately said.

'Off the record, I was contacted by a senior person in the judicial system, who told me, there was no need to attend that day, in Rahane, as the case had been settled out of court, it was only days afterwards, that a colleague told me of the contrary.

'It was a good thing, that you had the legal training and an eye for justice.' He continued, 'So I knew that somebody with influence in Rahane, tried to pervert the course of justice.

When I heard that this same gentleman, Mister O' Donoghue, was in need of defence, I agreed to act, even though I had retired from capital cases. Therefore, I hope you understand my absence on that occasion and by way of compensation and consolation, I promise that I will expend every drop of blood to make sure that Mister O' Donoghue, here gets a proper defence.

Although I will admit that an eyewitness and the lack of cooperation from my client are making things very difficult.'

He continued in a forlorn mode, 'I will also tell you that unless we produce some rabbit from a hat, things are looking bleak. I wish he would confide in me, not just constantly claiming his innocence.'

'Do you mind if I try?' I asked He punched me lightly on the shoulder, as he vacated his chair and went to stand by the door.

I met Willie near the window, and I bombarded him, instantly with questions.

Why was he not declaring innocence, why did he hide the gun and why did he think he would not be convicted.

Throughout the tirade, he looked at me with a very confused look. Eventually he looked at Mister Hay, to confirm permission to speak.

He said, 'I didn't want you, getting the blame he said, and you as good as gold ta us.'

I immediately sat him down on the chair, and spoke condescendingly to him.

'Willie, from the top, now I want the full story.'

As he spoke, it was becoming apparent to me now as to the reason for his silence.

'Well,' he stuttered, 'I was heading to a job, early de morning after de auction, as I walked passed de church. I saw de fella dat delivers de morning papers, knockin at de window of your jeep, he taut you were dead, but when he saw you movin he said, 'Tank God, I tought it was another murder.'

I axed him what he ment and he told me dat Josie O 'Leary was shot last night, outside his house.

I knew you done it and so I drove you home, den I carried ya into de room and den I took away de gun and hid it cause I knew de police might come looking for ya. We understood why ya done cause you liked our Rosie nearly more dan we did. Meself and Kathleen, was glad dat dey arrested me, instead of you. Cause we knew I didn't do it.'

'Glad?!' I shouted. 'You poor, fool! Do you know unless we can think of something fast you are likely to get twenty years in gaol.'

For the first time, I saw the reality; instil a panic in his mind.

'But I know I didn't do it,' he repeated with such an innocence on his face that defied logic.

'Why will I go to gaol?' He bemused, thinking in his childish state that somehow if he is not guilty some miraculous aura will enter the courtroom and instruct the jury to acquit him.

I replied in a tone that was intended to shock him to reality, 'Because sometimes the law is an ass and mistakes are made. All some of these people want is a person to blame, it does not matter if you are guilty or not.'

Willie sat down in the chair, placed his head in his large hands and cried. I was about to kneel down and attempt some form of consolation gesture but Mister Hay stopped me and asked me to recount my involvement pertaining to the location of the weapon.

He was definitely intrigued about the amount of cartridges and seemed quietly confident about his next course of action.

'The only thing we have to watch now is where Willie's innocence will lead if in fact I do prove him innocent.'

Before these words made any further impact, the guard, returned and said, 'Come Sir,' as he pointed to Willie, 'The time is up to return, the judge will be back in three minutes.'

Coskin and the barrister were deep in

discussion on our walk back to the courtroom about the layout of the drive and forecourt of the O' Leary household and in connection with this Coskin handed Mister Hay a photograph.

When the court re-convened, Mister Hay immediately stood up and made his opening statement.

'Ladies and gentlemen of the jury, contrary to what you have been told, this is far from a simple case. This is in fact a very, complex case. A case, where the loyalty of one man, was so great as to put himself forward to take the blame for another. It is a story that shows the genuine care and loyalty of a man that my learned friend tried to portray as evil.

'Just like him, as he points to the prosecutor, 'I too… Have no personal knowledge of the victim in this case, so I will not make random judgements about his or anyone else's character. I will be calling various witnesses to do that for me.

Therefore, I ask you as a first step towards justice, to make decisions for yourselves. Do not accept hearsay, even if the conveyor is wearing a uniform. We are dealing with a man's life and freedom here, so I urge you to deal in facts. In addition, may I point out that, the issue of my client being a member of the travelling community is of no significance in this case.

He like you and I, is a human being, and at this moment that is all you can say about him with absolute conviction. He is innocent until proven guilty. Therefore, I ask you all to please, listen carefully to the evidence and if there is the slightest doubt in any of your minds, as to his guilt, then I ask you to return a verdict in keeping with your conviction. Thank you.

The judge then asked the prosecutor to call his next witness.

'I call, Misses Noreen O Leary".

It was the first time that I had actually seen Misses O' Leary up close. I thought to myself as she was sworn in, that she was indeed as Coskin had described, a large physical looking woman with glasses. She had long, fiery, red hair and a disposition to match.

'Now Misses O Leary, could you tell us the circumstances, surrounding the events on the night of your husband's brutal murder.'

'I can', she said, 'At about twelve o clock I heard the dogs barking. When I ran outside, I saw Josie walking up the drive. Just as he got past the last scrapped car that was nearest to the house, this guy jumped out and shot him. He was standing only a foot from his face, shot him he did.... not once but many times. He turned around and he looked at me, and then put the gun down by his side and just walked off down by the passage. As soon as he left I rushed to poor Josie, but shure he was dead as a Christmas turkey.'

A slight murmur of laughter, trickled around the silence, but a frown from the judge, quelled it as fast as it started.

'He was dead I tell ya,' she continued, 'blood running from his face.'

'Now I know this is hard for you', the prosecutor suggested.

'Did you get a good look at the murderer?'

'I did…' 'Are you certain?'

'Yes I am,' was the prearranged symphony.

'Is that man in court today?'

She pointed straight down to Willie and she said, 'That's him, that's the tinker!'

The prosecutor turned to the judge and then to the jury, he smiled as he said, 'No further question, Your Honour.'

Mr Hay then stood up and he said to the woman.

'Hello Misses O' Leary, can you tell me a few things first about your husband. Was he a good husband?'

'Yes he was', she said, 'the best.'

'What did he work at?' Was the next question from the defence.

'Well … he didn't work at all.. .'

She said in an apologetically fashion, 'He hurt his back some time ago and he hasn't worked since, not this long time.'

'Can you tell the court where he was coming from on the night of the incident?'

'He … well … he … he … went down for a walk, just down to the village.'

'How long had he been gone for this walk?'

'No more than an hour or so I would reckon.'

'So you're telling the court that he was not in the pub drinking all day?'

'Objection!' Was the immediate response from the prosecution, 'Does it matter whether Mr O Leary was drinking or was drunk? The main fact was that he was shot in cold blood.'

Mister Hay turned around and said, 'Excuse me, Superintendent, that is for the jury to decide, not you.'

The judge instructed Miss O Leary to answer the question, she said, 'yeah, he probably had a drink or two at the pub.'

Mr Hay said, 'I put it to you that he was gone all day in fact, was he not?

'Am…well I was busy around the house, I didn't notice as to whether he had been in the house during the day, he was around somewhere, he could have been next door at our neighbours. He spends a lot of time there, him and Peadar Scanlon are good friends.'

'Come on now Miss O Leary, I am quite certain that you knew he was in the pub all day and in fact that is where he would spend most of his days isn't it?'

How many children do you have?' He continued.

'Seven', she replied.

'Are they boys or girls?' He asked.

'Five girls and two boys,' she replied.

'Now tell this court, was Mister O' Leary, ever intimate with any of them?'

Before she got a chance to answer, I

thought the judge would explode as he castigated Mister Hay for asking such a question. He instructed Misses O' Leary to ignore the question and he gave a similar instruction to the jury.

The purpose of this strategy by Mister Hay was I assumed, to try to paint a picture to the jury of the real, O' Leary.

'Did you love your husband?' Was the next question, This time the superintendent rose. 'Objection, your honour! This has no relevance whatsoever to the case," The judge looked at Mister Hay and said, "Yes Mr Hay, I am afraid we will have to overrule that question," "I'm sorry, Your Honour", was his instant reply as he continued.

'Now you said that the dogs barking brought you to the front door, would the dogs always bark, when Mister O' Leary returned from anywhere?'

'Yes, they were always glad to see him,' 'So, let me understand this, every time Mister O' Leary came home the dogs barked?'

'Yes,' she said.

'And every time the dogs barked you got up from watching television or whatever you were doing and went outside the front door, is that right?'

'No don't be silly,' she said, 'If I went outside every time the dogs barked I might as well live outside.'

'So then we are safe to say, that on the

night in question, it was more likely to be the gun shots that made you go outside, is that not a more reasonable assumption?'

'Well, whatever,' she replied, 'I still saw the fella who shot him.'

'That may be so,' Hay continued, 'but if the gunshots alerted you and the act was already committed, I doubt if the shooter, would stand around and wait until you came out, given that there are also three other houses nearer to him.

So, on that basis, I suggest that you did not see anybody out there or even if you did he or she was so far out of your sight, it would make identification impossible?'

'I tell you, I know what I saw and it was him, the tinker sitting at that table over there.' She shouted.

Unperturbed, Hay continued, 'I notice you wear glasses, Misses O' Leary, so I hope you don't mind if I carry out a little experiment in a moment.'

He turned to the jury and said, 'I can call a reliable witness later to verify the distances that I am about to quiz Misses O' Leary on.

In the meantime I would like you to persevere with my mode of questioning.'

He turned once again to the witness, 'I have a photo of your front driveway, firstly I would like you to take a good look at it Misses O' Leary, and verify that it is a recent photograph of your house and can you further, verify that it is a true likeness of your driveway and forecourt.'

She looked at the photograph, quite dismissively and without even thinking any further, she confirmed the claim of the questioner.

'Yeah, that is our house alright.'

Hay continued. 'Now, you see that scrapped car in the foreground?

'Is this where the perpetrator jumped from?'

Again, she agreed.

'Now', he said, 'Can you tell me, from the front door of the house how far away is that car?'

She replied in an arrogant tone, 'I don't know distances, but it's not very far.'

'Not very far?' As he spoke, he handed the Polaroid to the jury, for their perusal.

'Well then let me tell you,' he said. 'It is at least one hundred feet and believe me that is quite a distance.'

'If you say so.' Was the matter of fact reply.

'Now, what I am going to do is, to introduce you to my assistant,' he summoned his clerk to his side.

'Misses O' Leary, this young lad's name is Rory. Now I have asked Rory and some members of the public to stand at the end of this courtroom and what I want you to do is this, before Rory takes up that position I want you to take a good look at him. I want you to look closely until you are absolutely sure that you would recognise him again if you saw him. Right are you happy with the familiarity of his face?'

'Yes sir, I would know him again if I saw him.' She confirmed.

Mister Hay then instructed his clerk to leave the courtroom and to return in a line up with three others.

Three of the men in the line up were wearing Arran sweaters; one was wearing a shirt and a tie. The simple alteration, Mister Hay, had made was that his clerk on exiting the courtroom was wearing a collar and a tie, but once outside the door he pulled on a sweater. The exchange had been completed in the briefest of time and the witness did not see through the ruse.

'Now Misses O' Leary which of these three men is the man I introduced to you at close range moments ago?'

Without a moments hesitation she pointed to the collar and tie chap.

Hay called him forward and as he got closer, it was now becoming obvious that she had called it incorrectly.

'Okay,' Hay continued. 'Let me explain to you what just happened here.

Misses O' Leary, from where you are currently seated, the distance to the entrance door is approximately, seventy feet.

We are also further graced with electric light that already compliments all the natural light that enters this room through the large magnificent windows all around us.

Your driveway does not I assume have such lucidity, especially at twelve o clock at night. So I put it to you, that how in the name of God could you positively identify a figure in the dark at one hundred feet when in fact you failed to identify a man at a lesser distance in significantly better lighting conditions?'

'It was him I tell you,' as she repeatedly pointed at Willie.

'It had to be him; no one else had any reason to kill Josie. That tinker had it in for him; he blamed Josie for messing with his girl.'

Mister Hay then played the tactful card.

'Misses O' Leary, I know this is rough and difficult for you, but can you understand that there is a possibility that you were mistaken and I understand how that could happen, especially if you believed that Willie O' Donoghue was the only person likely to harm your husband. So we all understand if you made a mistake, all we need you to say is that you are not positive as to the identity of the stranger on that night.'

'Objection,' was the instant reply from the prosecution, 'Mister Hay is leading the witness.'

'Overruled,' was the verdict of the judge.

Hay continued, 'Misses O' Leary, on behalf of the jury, I must ask you are you still sure of the identity of the man you saw killing your husband?'

She broke into a soft crying mood but the entire court heard her say through the sobbing, 'No I am not sure. Can I sit down now?'

Mister Hay escorted her from the witness stand, as he declared, 'No further questions.'

Immediately the prosecution called the coroner to verify the cause and nature of the death. After he had stated the facts that we already knew, he was asked to identify the calibre of the shells that caused the fatality.

'I removed five different bullets all fired from the same gun at very close range, they were fired from a 303 calibre gun.'

'Is this the gun that fired the bullets?' The inspector continued.

'Yes,' was the reply from the coroner.

'No further questions,' was the prosecution chant as he returned to his seat.

Mister Hay bolted from his seat at a rate that defied his age.

'Doctor, can I ask you to please tell the court when did you qualified as a medical practitioner?'

'In nineteen forty six,' was the confident reply from the witness. 'The fourteenth of June to be exact.'

'Good,' replied Mister Hay, 'now can you tell us when you qualified as a ballistics expert?'

'I don't know what you mean.' He replied.

'Allow me to explain,' Hay continued, 'Or better still let me ask you the same question that you were asked by my colleague. Is this the gun that fired the bullets that you removed from the body of Josie O' Leary? Let me remind you that your answer on that occasion was, yes.

Now I ask you once again the same question.' This time the coroner was a lot clearer in his answer,' It was a gun with the same bore as that one.'

'So to clarify further,' Hay continued, 'there is absolutely nothing, in your opinion that links that gun to the murder other than the model, is there?'

'Nothing', was the sheepish reply. It was now becoming obvious that the prosecution were starting to panic; their case was unravelling before them. I expected them to call Willie as I thought they would see him as their vulnerably prey, in an attempt to redress the hammering they were receiving.

Nothing could have prepared me for the next call, 'Your Honour, we would like to call Jonathan Rogers.'

I was expecting to be summoned at some stage, but even when the call came; it still hit me as a shock.

As I walked down the stairs and entered the main room, I asked my 'Angel' to help me to say the right things and not to do Willie's cause any harm.

The 'swearing in', was a blur as I felt a further tinge of pain down my side probably brought on by the current tension.

The prosecutor started his tirade immediately, 'Mister Rogers, can you identify this weapon and could you tell the court the model and the cartridges required to render it active?'

I agreed that it was in fact my gun and I confirmed that the bore was a 303. He then asked me to explain the reason that the detectives could not find it when they searched my property the morning after the shooting and how did I knew where to locate it.

I said, 'When I called to see Willie O' Donoghue at the gaol in Limerick, he told me where he had hidden it.'

'Did you not think it was suspicious, that a man was killed using a gun of the same calibre as this, then someone, who is a prime suspect in the murder confided in you as to the whereabouts of the weapon?' He probed.

'The reason for this...' I started to reply, but he interjected immediately, 'I will ask you again Mister Rogers, did you not think it suspicious?'

I replied, 'At the time yes, but…' Again he interrupted in an arrogant staccato tone, 'That will be all Mister Rogers.'

He then turned to the jury, and said, 'Let me explain my understandable, confusion.

For many years, a gun lay over the mantle of a house, a simple ornament, causing no harm to man or beast. Then we have a fatal shooting, an innocent family man was gunned down. The gun used in the assassination was a gun such as this,' he reinforced his words by raising the gun aloft, as he continued.

'Then the very same day this gun, not any other gun disappeared, the only man in this tightly knit community that harboured a grudge against the victim, was the only man who knew the location of its hiding place. His best friend in the neighbourhood has openly admitted here in this courtroom, that even he thinks it is suspicious.

To hide something from the police is also suspicious, so I put it to you that this act is, indeed above the realm of suspicion.

It is, in fact an admission of guilt.

No further questions.'

CHAPTER 43

At this juncture, the judge suggested to all that it was time for a lunch break. He instructed the jury to follow an usher of the court to a small hotel across the road, where a private room had been reserved for their lunch, he further instructed them to desist from discussing the case with any third party and completed his instruction by telling me I was still under oath and was to return to the witness stand at two o' clock sharp.

Coskin, Hay, his clerk and I met in the foyer and from there we headed to a local restaurant. I struggled to consume a bowl of soup, whilst the others had a substantial meal.

Mister Hay gave his verdict on the progress of the case and reiterated what was obvious to me that my testimony to date was the only 'straw the prosecution had to clutch at.'

I apologised for coming across as a wimp, but he assured me that the nature of the questioning would have brought the same result from anybody.

'The only thing none of us have addressed', he continued, Is that the definitive proof of innocence is to suggest or identify the true murderer.'

He opened his leather organiser to write some notes as he was speaking.

Coskin admitted that although many claims were made in the courtroom as to the likeability of O' Leary, 'There were a lot more people who disliked him. As to who would wish him harm I cannot imagine. In actual fact, he only had a small circle of friends.'

To which I added, 'even less friends than maybe he realised himself,' I referred to the conversation I had with Peadar Scanlon, by the men's room door, the night of the murder.

At this point Coskin leaned across the table and quite cheekily removed the photo of the O' Leary house, that lay on top of the pile of papers in Hay's folder.

It was definitely a eureka moment, 'That's it, Damm it, that … is … it.' He shouted.

We looked at him with a form of stare one would associate with 'rabbits in the headlights.'

'Okay, let me give you all some facts and add in a little conjecture, 'We know that O' Leary left the pub at around ten o clock, however he did not get home 'til midnight.

Let us suppose, he somehow heard you and Scanlon talking. Johnny, you said, that he had threatened to harm Scanlon's young daughter if it became public knowledge of the attack on the O' Donoghue campsite, then, some time before mid night, Peadar Scanlon's young daughter was rushed to Limerick general.

You also said John, that you saw her

parents, coming from the intensive care unit. We also know that there was no immediate taxi available to take you home on the night in question, so equally there was no taxi to allow Scanlon to follow his family, he could not use his own car as O'Leary had the keys.'

When I met him later on that night, while investigating the shooting he volunteered information regarding his daughter falling down two flights of stairs. This now turns out to be a distraction tactic, to divert my attention from what had really happened.'

'Hay immediately said,' Sorry Mick you have lost me...' 'Misses O' Leary,' Coskin continued, 'said in the witness stand that her husband spends a lot of his time next door at Scanlon's house.'

'So...' Mister Hay asked quizzing him further.

'In this photo you can see a perfect picture of the house next door; it is in fact a bungalow. It does not have, **one**, not to mention **two**, flights of stairs.'

'Are you suggesting, that O' Leary carried out some sort of physical abuse on the young girl?' Mister Hay enquired.

'Well, you asked for an alternative suspect to Willie O' Donoghue, there you have one.' Coskin concluded.

'Right then,' said Hay, 'the next thing to do is when I cross examine you, Johnny, in the witness stand on our return, I will have to ask you about your conversation with Scanlon and the threat made by O' Leary. I want to warn you now however it still could go *pear shaped* if you are not believed. Ideally, we need a medical report on the injuries to the young girl, but they can only be subpoenaed by the court if the parents were to object, as I am sure they will.

It is without question that both her parents are aware of what happened on that night and there is every possibility they will corroborate each other's story. So as it will be two of them against your word, you may not be believed.

The main purpose, however,' he continued, 'of this exercise is to create doubt as to the guilt of Willie, as for how the Scanlon's deal with the accusations, or how the law deals with them is not our direct concern.'

Coskin, however took a different approach as he had to act on the probabilities before him and to make sure that the information he possessed about a violent person did not turn nasty, he took the unprecedented step of taking a seat beside Peadar Scanlon as no one could predict what was about to happen, once the questioning began.

Somehow, I knew it was a catch twenty-two situation, I had to save Willie but by so doing, I am possibly going to exile Scanlon to a life behind bars. I was really trying to remain focused on the situation, but there were many times when my mind drifted and I had to bring myself back to the task in hand.

I was once again reminded about being under oath, as the court resumed. I could not help myself staring over at Mister and Misses Scanlon, knowing that their lives were about to change.

'Mister Rogers,' was the opening cry from Hay. 'Can you tell the court any reason as to why you think Mister O' Donoghue, is not guilty of this crime?

My thoughts were swirling around in my head. I knew this was my last chance to clear Willie. I remember thinking, 'God forgive me and more importantly help me. It is now time to find my true self after being lost for so long.

I turned to the judge and I asked him for permission to approach Garda Coskin. He was rather taken back by this request, but agreed. The expression on all others in the courtroom especially Mister Hay was one of total confusion.

I slowly walked to where Coskin was sitting and placed my face about ten inches from Peadar Scanlon's. I said, 'How is your little girl, how serious are her injuries?'

He was about to deny me access to any information, but his wife looked in to my eyes and again I thanked god for women's intuition.

She whispered the words that changed my view on the extent of barbaric acts that one man could inflict on another. Further it convinced me that what I was about to do, was the better of two evils.

'She is badly torn up inside, her uterus and intestines are torn beyond repair, she will never be without an incontinence bag and will never bear a child.'

The last part of this sentence was 'gut wrenching not just for her, but for her husband and me alike. I reached out and held her hand as she cried convulsively.

'Objection, Your Honour,' the prosecution cried, 'do we need this charade?'

I slowly returned to the witness stand and took many deep breaths. Then I continued.

'You asked me Mister Hay as to why I thought Mister O' Donoghue was innocent of the crime, well I want to tell the court that I know with an absolute degree of certainty that Willie, was prepared to admit to this crime for the reasons you outlined during your opening statement.

Yes, he was prepared to take the fall for me.

You see a few months ago I met a young girl called Rosie O' Donoghue, Willie's daughter.

Yes, she was only eleven years old and I was old enough to be her grandfather, but the relationship we formed stepped outside all conventional boundaries. As to the rights and wrongs of this unity, it is for every individual looking on, to independently assess.

She became a vital part of my life, she brought sunshine and happiness, like I had never experienced. She was an angel in a human body. I am not ashamed to announce here today that I fell in love with her, she was beautiful, she was innocent and she was perfect.

However, these qualities did not go unnoticed, by others. She attracted the attention of Josie O' Leary, a cruel and evil man, who through hatred and revenge took the life of this gem.

By so doing, he broke the hearts of her parents, her brothers and me.

Because of this act, I took it upon myself to confront him at his house and with that gun there, I sent him to answer to his maker.

You asked me how I know Willie O' Donoghue, did not commit this crime.

This is how I know.'

CHAPTER 44

As I lie here in the prison infirmary, the overhead lights are dimming and brightening, mirroring the feebleness of my life.

I have had a wonderful life, a life that had two beginnings. I came to Ireland to find a piece of Heaven, but Heaven found me.

I am ready to go now, so does it really matter what other mortals think of me? I am comforted when I recall those words of Kathleen O' Donoghue.

'She died to be wit you, in a place where no one will be judging or no one will be judged.'

As I grip my precious flower, I ask for the last time.

Angel Rosie lets dance.

I feel very uncomfortable having to share a world with those who go from the cradle to the grave judging others, while at the same time never getting to know themselves.

For more information and other works by this author, visit www.cathalokeeney.co.uk